Kendall Evone Hayes

SEASONS *of* HOPE

Kendall evone Hayes

SEASONS

of HOPE

HER Healed Empowered Restored
1601 E. Mt. Airy Ave Ste 201B
Phila., PA 19150

Ordering Information:
Quantity sales. Special discounts are available on quantity purchases by corporations, associations, and others. For details, contact the publisher at the address above.
Orders by U.S. trade bookstores and wholesalers. Please contact HER Healed Empowered Restored: Tel: 267-593-7604

Printed in the United States of America

ISBN-13:978-1530354740

ISBN-10:1530354749

CONTENTS

PREFACE

One of the fundamental ingredients for a wholesome mar- riage—or for any healthy relationship whether it be mother and son, brother or sister or friendships with those outside our family—is honesty.

With this in mind, the fundamental issue behind Kendall Hayes's book *Season of Hope* isn't that of homosexuality; whether or not homosexuality is right or wrong, whether they should be permitted to marry or not, that has no relevance to the story in which Hayes tell. Some might try to read this into her writings for their own personal reasons or seek to twist her intentions to make it seem as if the topic of the book has to do with the homosexuality of one of its characters, but that would be not only incorrect, but it also would be yet another missed opportunity for open and honest discussion on a very important issue.

It is such honest discussion that is sorely missing in our com- munities today. Think about it: When was the last time your church, synagogue, or *masjid* had spoken about the role of mar- riage as related to homosexuality? What about your friends, those in your peer group?

When I say "discuss the issue," I do not mean having some superficial and momentary discussion about homosexual and heterosexual relationships but a deeper, more balanced evaluation of the subject from both sides of the coin, meaning from a gay and straight perspective. You have probably not had such discus- sions or, if you have, very few.

Yet we need to do so. Faith-based groups shy away from the topic and just make a stand one way or another according to their traditions and beliefs, and that is that. Our friends might men- tion it as a conversation piece; state their formed opinion, prob- ably laced with lewd jests, without any significant exploration of the matter; and move on to the next topic.

However, there are gay people who are married or in relation- ships with straight people who have no idea that their significant other or spouse is attracted to members of the same sex or, for that matter, gay people in relationships with someone whom they did not know were straight.

This is why of *Seasons of Hope* is such an important book; it brings to the light that which we have left lurking in the shadows far too long; it raises an important issue that we have publicly ignored and socially suppressed far too many times.

My hope is that after you read the book, you will discuss it with your friends, family members, and those in the groups and organizations where you belong.

This fascinating book is more than just a good read, but it is also a step towards the light.

—Nathaniel Lee

Season of Loss

Hope was so tired. Her husband, John, had been sleeping on the couch for a whole year. They hardly spoke to each other, but each morning he got up, took the kids to school, and arrived at their place of business. He acted as if life at home was fine. They continued to conduct and run their business effec- tively, and no one in the office would ever suspect that their mar- riage was on the brink. She prayed every morning that things would get better, but for the past two years things seemed to have gotten worse.

Hope didn't fully understand what happened to cause her marriage to be in such a state of disaster, but she knew that she would no longer allow herself to be verbally abused. So she lim- ited her communication with John and acquainted herself with him only on subjects that involved their children. She didn't real- ize that her actions would make the emotional and psychologi- cal abuse worse than ever. She built up a wall around her emo- tions trying to keep the abuse from penetrating into her psyche, but deep down inside she was dying, and she didn't know how much longer she could take it. She felt like she was going to lose her mind.

❦

To the outside world, John was a highly respected business- man, church deacon, dedicated father, and loving husband who lived in a $300,000-dollar home in the suburbs of Philadelphia. To their church family, he was a devoted husband, father, and a faithful deacon who lavished his wife with expensive gifts. This was his family church, and these people knew John since he was a baby. He could do no wrong in their eyes. To them, everything about John was perfect. They saw him as the man to aspire to become if you were a boy and the perfect man to be with if you were a woman.

Hope joined his church when they got married. She had always loved the Lord and wanted to always do what is pleasing in his sight. So when she found a church-going man, she thought she had found her perfect mate. Hope conformed to the lifestyle with John and was very happy at first. She was active in church, and they attended as a perfectly happy family every week. Hope sang on the choir, worked in women's ministry, and was active with all the girls' activities in church and school. She wanted her girls to have the lifestyle that she'd always wanted: a two-parent home. Her dad died when she was three, and Hope was raised by her grandmother. She and her mother, Bernie, had just become close after the birth of her daughter Kennedy. Bernie was a great g'mom, making up for the time lost raising Hope.

Yes, to the outside world, Hope's life was perfect. No one knew that Hope wore a mask every day, trying to keep up appearances. John got angry when she didn't keep up appearances. Appearance meant everything to John. Everyone around them had to think they had the perfect family, and John was the "king of the hill." He expressed his undying love and devotion for her in public, but at home he was quite a different person—a distant stranger full of anger and hostility toward her for reasons that were unbe- known to her.

The highly successful businessman to the outside world was not a good provider for his family. Although his salary from their business was $90,000 per year, Hope repeatedly came home to a house where, on any given day, the electricity, gas, phones, and water would be shut off. The lavish gifts that he bestowed upon his wife for the pubic to ogle over were always purchased on credit cards that she ended up paying. Her salary was only $40,000 per year, yet she did most of the work at the company and at home. She learned that somehow she had to manage to keep all the utilities on, keep their two kids in private school, and maintained the household on her salary alone. At times she had to ask her mom for assistance, despite the fact that John's salary was adequate for him to take care of his family. She didn't know what he did with his money and learned not to ask. Even so, she still loved John. For her "I do" meant for a lifetime. She made excuses for him when she had to ask her mom for help, hoping that he would come around and be the man she knew he could be.

She never let the kids know that things were bad. On birth- days and holidays, she and her mom always made sure the kids had everything they wanted and more. Hope always made the kids believe that all gifts came from Daddy and Mommy. She did not want to tarnish their view of their father. It was important to Hope that the kids have a positive image of a father figure because she never had that while she was growing up. She was determined that her girls would have a positive father figure in the home—even if she had to fabricate a lie.

God only knew where John's money went because she never saw a dime of it, and he hardly paid any bills. If it wasn't for her mother, she wouldn't have been able to maintain. Bernie never really cared for John but never showed it; she just did whatever she could. Only once did she share her disdain for John, but after seeing the pained look on her daughter's face, she never said another word against her daughter's husband. She understood

how much Hope loved him, so she just supported Hope's decisions. That was just one of the ways she tried to make up for childhood mishaps between her and Hope. Besides, she had lived long enough to know that when a woman loves a man, there's nothing that nobody can say that will change the way she feels.

But now Hope was truly tired. She'd finally had enough. She knew that she served a God who did not want her to be unhappy. As much as she was against divorce, she knew she had to do something. The stress was beginning to wear her down; she now had hypertension and had to take three medications every day. Her hair was graying, and she always felt and looked worn down. She was sure John was having an affair, with all his late-night business meetings along with the fact that they hadn't touched each other in over a year; but still she needed proof. She decided to hire a private investigator.

The next morning, John said nothing as usual. Hope noticed that he was wearing a new suit. She thought of how many bills he could have paid with the money he spent on that suit. All of his suits were tailored made and ranged from $500–$800, depending on the material and linings. Yeah, he could have paid a few bills with that money he was wearing on his back. It didn't matter to him that his family was going to be in the dark as long as he looked good to the outside world. Hope said nothing as she put the latest shutoff notice from the electric company on the dining room table where she was sure he would see it.

Today was the day. She finally decided to hire a private investigator so she would have proof of John's infidelity. Maybe the proof would give her the courage to finally file for divorce. But deep down inside she didn't want to be alone; divorce would be a very hard and unfamiliar territory for her and the kids. She knew John would fight her tooth and nail; but she couldn't continue to live like this. She needed the proof.

As soon as John and the kids left the house, Hope showered and got dressed. She chose one of the many black suits that hung in her closet. Yes, she had many suits—all of them dark colored and of good quality. She was lucky to be a size 10 because the thrift stores always had nice things in her size. Not one of her suits cost more than $25. She got dressed and got her notepad where she had written down the name and address of a local private investigator. This particular morning she didn't even pray. She purposely didn't answer the phone when her prayer partner called. She was tired of praying every day with her prayer partner, and her life seemed to get progressively worse while her prayer partner's life seemed almost perfect. They say birds of a feather flock together, so Hope often wondered if her prayer partner's perfect life was like her own life—a complete lie. Could her prayer partner also be wearing a mask? No, today she decided not to have prayer. When she called, the PI asked if she could come in to his office that morning. She arrived within the hour.

"Good morning, Mrs. Darroff. I'm Peter Hampton, PI. Thanks for coming in. Have a seat."

Hope had only spoken to the man an hour earlier, and here she was in his office, ready to have him spy on her husband. Oddly enough, she felt comfortable. The office was small but cozy, clean, and well furnished. Mr. Hampton was a short balding man with a firm handshake and good eye contact.

"So, you think your husband is having an affair. What makes you think that?" he asked.

Hope took a deep breath before she began her story. "We haven't touched each other in over a year. He sleeps on the couch, and we hardly talk at home. He always has late-night 'meetings' and is very distant toward me."

"Hmmm. So tell me, Mrs. Darroff, if your husband hasn't been talking to you and hasn't been intimate with you for over a

Year, why are you just now deciding to investigate him? I mean, it seems to me like you would have started an investigation nine or ten months ago."

Hope thought about that. It was a good question, but it caught her off guard. She bounced back quickly. "Well, to be perfectly honest, I welcomed the lack of communication and intimacy. It was far better than his constant belittling and verbal abuse. And the intimacy, well, let's just say the two- to five-minute sessions lacked substance."

"I see. Okay. I'll need you to fill out these forms, and I'll need a recent photo of your husband; a $1,000 deposit and I can get started right away, Mrs. Darroff."

Hope felt much lighter, like a heavy burden had been lifted. Finally she would learn the truth. She had a pretty good idea of who John was having an affair with. It was no secret that he'd had a fling with his assistant. She started walking around the office acting like *she* was Mrs. Darroff, so he put an end to that. He couldn't have his facade of a marriage unmasked. She had forgot- ten the rules of the game. Hope also suspected he was having a love affair with an attorney at the law firm of Jonas and Smith. There were several calls to that office on his cell phone bill, but this was not their attorney. The calls were always around 5:00 p.m. There were several calls made to a number that she tracked to Atty. S. L. Wright. Probably some attorney who worked for the firm.

Time would soon reveal the truth, she thought as she got into her car. She decided to go to the office after all.

As she drove, she began to try to figure out how she had got- ten to this point. When did John stop loving her? They were mar- ried when Kennedy was two years old. She was the primary rea- son for the marriage—for both her and John. They were young: John, twenty; and Hope, twenty-three. But they both wanted their daughter to have a chance at a functional family life, com-

plete with a mommy and daddy under the same roof. She was determined to keep her family together and make any necessary sacrifices that would allow her daughter to have a normal family life. Two years later, she got pregnant with their second daughter, Kamari. The first time John hit her was during that pregnancy.

They received the first of many shutoff notices for the elec- tric, which she thought John had been paying. The bill was four months behind. Hope didn't want to bother John with the news because he was always so irritable when he came home from work. So she prepared his favorite meal: salmon, mashed potatoes, and asparagus. As soon as he got home, she served him dinner and let him eat in peace. Once she cleaned up the kitchen, bathed Kennedy, and put her to bed, she went into the living room and gave John the shutoff notice.

He exploded. "What the fuck do you want me to do?"

"Well, I thought you were paying the electric all this time. I've been paying the mortgage, water, phone—"

Slap! He slapped Hope across the left side of her face with the front of his hand and then quickly slapped the other side of her face with the back of his hand. It happened so fast that Hope didn't even have a chance to remind him of all the other bills she paid. She was so stunned and afraid that she didn't utter another word.

"Well then, you can pay the damn electric bill too, bitch. You got everything under control, right? Pay the damn bill. And that electric better not get shut off either!" Then he stormed out of the house.

Hope's hands were shaking as she reached into the freezer to get some ice. She wrapped some cubes in a dishtowel and put it on her face. She convinced herself that it was her fault that John hit her. She *made* him do it. She should have just handled the situation herself and not bothered him with it. He had so many other things on his mind. He always told her how hard it was— being a black man trying to make it in this world. She promised God she would do better when it concerned him.

She should have left him then, but she didn't. After Kamari was born, Hope received a large settlement from an automobile accident. She agreed to put a substantial down payment on a home in Lavock. John had always wanted to live there, so when he told her about the house he found, she thought it would be a good start for them. The mortgage payment was only $600 per month. John was working steadily as an electrician, so the plan was to live off his salary so Hope could be a stay-at-home mom. She performed some consulting work on the side, and after about four years she was making a substantial income while being home with the kids. It seemed to be the perfect arrangement. Thinking back, she realized that John had always made disappearing acts on her. She never paid it much attention because she was busy being a wife and mother, maintaining her home and raising her children. There were many nights when she had no idea what time John arrived home because she would be sound asleep.

Their sex life had never been very exciting. John could only last about three to seven minutes and afterward would imme- diately get up, go wash himself off, jump back in the bed, turn his back on her, and fall fast asleep. She knew exactly what Miss Celie from *The Color Purple* meant when she said, "Mister just got on top of me and did his business." That's exactly what John did. Got on top of her and did his business. No foreplay for her at all.

She always had orgasm, but still, there was no cuddling or even any communication afterward. Then there were those disap- pearing acts. There had always been something unsettling. Hope just couldn't put her finger on it. God had given her many gifts, but discernment was not one of them.

Her mind jumped back to the present as she pulled up into the parking lot. As soon as she got into her office and began checking her voice mails, there was a knock on the door.

"Come in."

It was Sharon, John's assistant. "Excuse me, Mrs. Darroff, but John has been looking for you all morning. He wants to see you in his office immediately."

"Okay, Sharon," Hope replied. "Close the door on your way out." Just the sight of that woman made Hope's skin crawl. Hope had long ago made it clear that they were not on a first-name basis. She called her Sharon, but under no circumstances was Sharon ever to call her by her first name. As for John, he'd have to wait until she finished checking her voice mails and enjoying her cup of coffee—or so she thought. Minutes later he came busting into her office.

"Where the hell have you been? And what have you been say- ing to Adam Strong? He refuses to meet with me unless you are present. I had a meeting scheduled with him this morning, but when he arrived and you weren't here, he wanted to reschedule. I've been trying to meet with him for months, and I finally get him in the office, and you're not here. When did you talk to him, and what the hell did you say that makes him speak so highly of you and only want to meet with me if you are present?"

"Well, good morning to you too, John. I've only been in Mr. Strong's presence on two occasions: at the mayor's birthday party and at the grand opening of the new art gallery in Center City. I guess he enjoyed our conversations. I didn't know you were meet- ing with him today; it wasn't on my schedule, and your assistant didn't inform me of the meeting."

John was fuming mad. "That's because I scheduled the meet- ing and did not include you. I didn't know how taken he was with you. No one knew where you were or even knew if you were coming in at all today. Your cell phone kept going straight to voice mail, and you couldn't be reached. Where were you?"

"I had a doctor's appointment."

John stared at Hope like he knew she was lying, then turned, and walked out the door. Then he came back and said, "I won't be home tonight."

Hope laughed to herself. *Good. Now, let the games begin.* She picked up the phone and called Mr. Hampton.

"Hello, Mr. Hampton? This is Mrs. Darroff. My husband just informed me that he won't be home tonight. Will you be able to begin following him tonight as soon as he leaves the office? Great! He usually leaves around 6:00 p.m."

Peter Hampton looked at the picture of John Darroff again. The face looked familiar. He was sure he'd seen John Darroff someplace. Yes, now he remembered. He'd seen him on several occasions at the bar on Eleventh and Locust. Peter frequented that bar himself looking to hook up with young men for sexual encounters on the down low. Mrs. Darroff was on the right track. Her husband was definitely cheating on her, but not with another woman. He was cheating with men.

This could be a goldmine, thought Peter. He would charge Mrs. Darroff up and then let Mr. Darroff know what was going on and extort money from him to keep his secret a secret. *Mrs. Darroff doesn't stand a chance at winning this one*, Peter thought. *She has no idea of how far the underground down low rabbit hole goes.* Yes, he would take the case and monitor Mr. Daroff's activities. Maybe he was having an affair with a woman, but he seriously doubted it. Mrs. Darroff was fine and sexy as hell. *Shit, if I were into women, I'd definitely do her myself*, he thought. But Peter was strictly dickly—all the way inside and out. He was curious how this situation would play out.

It had been two weeks since Hope hired Peter Hampton. She had heard from him twice, and that was only to say he needed more money for expenses. All in all she'd paid him $3,000 and had received not a shred of information. She was getting frustrated. John's late nights had become early mornings. She'd been trying to stay awake to see what time he came home, and he never got home before four thirty—sometimes as late as six, just in time to pretend he'd been home all night and get the kids up for school.

Hope wondered how long this had been going on. She hadn't been paying much attention because she was enjoying the peace of mind she had with him not being there; it helped limit the amount of communication she had with him. She assumed that he was just coming home late, waiting until he was sure she was asleep. Now she was absolutely sure he was having an affair, but she didn't say anything to him. He was short-tempered and was known to become physically and verbally abusive toward her. That's why she never said much to him and was glad that he'd stopped saying too much to her. At least that stopped the verbal abuse. But now she was enduring this emotional abuse, and she didn't know which was worse.

Hope's mother noticed how tired and worn she looked lately. As a mother (and a woman) she knew that something was ter- ribly wrong. She knew Hope would never admit it. She longed for the time when Hope would see her as a friend—not just a mother. She hated seeing her daughter like this, so she decided to schedule a vacation for Hope.

She got with Hope's cousin Patty, and they planned a four- day, three-night mini getaway to Paradise Island. Patty's mother was Bernie's sister, and Hope and Patty were more like sisters than cousins. They were complete polar opposites. Where Hope was a quiet homebody, mommy, and wife, Patty was the outgoing, opinionated career girl who always made her opinion heard.

Hope was actually looking forward to the vacation, although she was upset that they scheduled the trip without her knowl- edge. They had taken care of everything. The kids would stay with their g'mom. The airfare and hotel accommodations were paid for in full by the two of them. All Hope had to do was pack and arrive at the airport with spending money. Only two more days before her getaway and she hadn't told John yet. She planned to tell him today, probably while they were in the office, where it was safe.

When she arrived at the office, Sharon informed her that John and Adam Strong were in the conference room waiting for her. "Oh, okay. I didn't realize we had a meeting today. Did you send me an e-mail?"

"No, I didn't know about it until a few minutes ago myself, Mrs. Darroff."

Sharon has become more humble in the last few months. I guess John must have dumped her, and she sees just how much of an asshole he really is. Hope actually felt sorry for her—but only for a fleet- ing moment. She stopped in the ladies' room to check her make- up and hair before going into the meeting.

Mr. Strong was the CEO of one of the largest construction management companies in the northeast region. John had been trying to get an electrical contract with him for a few years now. This could be big! They surely needed the money. As it was, they were barely making payroll, and as owners, they were always last to get paid. It was now to the point where she was only being paid once a month, and most times it was still late, or short. Yes, thank God her mom and Patty scheduled this getaway! She could hardly wait. Okay. Make-up and hair look good. She still looked good despite what she'd been through and what she was going through.

"Well, good morning, honey," John said as he stood up and kissed her on the cheek.

Mr. Strong didn't miss the shocked look on Hope's face. He saw right through John Darroff. "Good morning, Mrs. Darroff. You look stunning as usual," he said as he placed her hand in both of his. He was a very handsome man.

Hope knew this meeting was very important to John. Maybe if they were able to get contracts with Mr. Strong, it would improve the condition of their marriage. Maybe he would be a positive influence on John since he and his wife had been married for about twenty years, and they seemed very happy.

"Thanks, Mr. Strong. You are too kind."

"Yes, my wife is very lovely indeed," John chimed in. "Now, let's get down to business, shall we? I understand that you have the contract for the airport expansion, Mr. Strong. I would like to bid the electrical contract."

"Yes, well, John, the specs for that project aren't even ready yet. You are way ahead of the game, my friend. That contract won't be out for bid for another two to three months. In the meantime, I suggest you start socializing with some of the bigwigs in the industry. Why don't you and your wife come over next weekend? My wife and I are having a small cocktail party, and there will be some very influential people there. We can talk more about other contracts then as well. That's how business is done on this level. We don't meet in board rooms to cut deals. Deals are cut at par- ties or on the golf course. Do you play golf, John?" John laughed.

"No, I don't have time. But I would love to learn."

"Well, why don't you come to the club this Saturday morning at six? We'll get you started."

Mr. Strong rose, indicating that he was finished with the meeting. "Well then, it was nice seeing you again, and I'm looking forward to forming a long and productive business relationship."

Adam kissed Hope on the cheek, shook John's hand, and left. John was ecstatic.

"Baby, we're on our way to the top! I'm taking you to lunch." He buzzed Sharon.

"Make lunch reservations for Mrs. Darroff and myself at Michelangelo's for 1:00 p.m."

"I have a few stops to make, but I'll meet you there at one. And, Hope, don't be late."

John arrived twenty minutes late. Hope had arrived fifteen minutes early and was on her third martini when he arrived. "Traffic is murder, and it's not even Friday yet. I need a vacation."

Hope chuckled, the martinis kicking in. "Funny you should mention vacations. I'm going away for a few days with Patty. My mom will have the kids so you'll be free for a few days as well."

Dead silence was John's initial response. Feeling the tension around her, Hope tensed up as the waitress appeared.

"Good afternoon, sir. Can I get you something to drink?" "Water with lemon,"

John replied. He prided himself on his

nonalcoholic intake and his healthy diet.

"Very good. Another martini for you, ma'am?"

"Yes, please."

John shook his head as the waitress departed to retrieve their drinks.

"So, when were you going to tell me about this…vacation you're going on, Hope? Or were you just going to leave me a note?" He didn't wait for a response. "Well, as haggard as you look, you probably need a vacation. Look at you. Your face is ashen and sunk in. You look like a piper. You hair is stringy and

oily. Yeah, you need it. I'm just curious as to how you paid for it when all the bills are overdue."

Hope chuckled again. "Patty and my mom paid for and arranged everything. Apparently they felt like I was in desperate need of a vacation too."

The waitress arrived with their drinks. "Are you ready to

order?"

"No. I'm late for a meeting and won't have time for lunch," he said as he threw a hundred-dollar bill on the table. He gave Hope a cold look and said, "This should cover her drinks and lunch. Enjoy, darling."

"That bitch," John said through clenched teeth as he made his way down Main

Street. *Who the hell do Patty and Bernie think they are arranging a vacation for Hope and no one bothered telling me? That shit burns me up*, he thought as he made his way into Hess Department Store. He maneuvered his way through the men's section downstairs to the men's room. He was so mad that he needed to release his frustration. He went into the last stall, dropped his pants, and put his penis into the hole that led to the adjacent stall and waited. In less than two minutes, he felt a warm, moist tongue licking his erect penis before sliding into a warm, moist mouth. He ejaculated in no time, pulled up his pants, and left feeling relieved. He never looked back to see who his anonymous server was. That was the beauty of this under- ground men-sexing-men secret hideaway. You never had to know who you had sex with. It was all about busting a nut and keeping it moving. It is said that this bathroom is frequented by men from all racial, cultural, and socioeconomic levels. John never looked at anyone straight in the eye. He wanted to remain anonymous. He did however glance the individual coming out of the stall from which he had just been serviced, but he quickly looked away.

John learned about this little secret rendezvous' spot while rendezvousing in the park one night. He was so frustrated with Hope after having a fight with her. Well, he did all the hollering and hitting. These fights were becoming more and more frequent and served as an excuse for him to leave the house and stay out late. He no longer liked having sex with Hope, and that added to his frustration. Coming home to her each night with her expect- ing him to have sex with her only gave him a reason to start a fight and storm out the house.

One particular night he drove to the park and just sat in his car. Before long a man pulled up beside him. They nodded at each other; then the guy came over to his car to ask for a light. John invited him to sit in the car with him, and in no time at all, the dude's hand went to John's crotch. John made no objections as the dude undid his pants and gave him an oral sex right there. He later told John that this spot was the spot where men came to have sex with each other. You could find a hookup in this section of the park at any time of day or night. It was one of the city's well-kept secrets and John's introduction to the yet another secret of the down-low brotherhood.

Adam Strong was sure to put his hat and sunglasses back on before leaving the bathroom stall. He often visited the stall at lunchtime. There was nothing like the sensation of a secret rendezvous to give you an adrenaline rush. Although a quickie, the gush of semen that he watched shoot out from the man's penis made him want to shoot his own load, and it gave him pleasure; and after giving some pleasure, he stayed to get a little pleasure of his own. He was not as quick as the one he serviced, but the release was just as powerful. He was sure he'd have a highly productive afternoon after this!

Hope was relieved when John left. She decided to have another martini and a salmon Caesar salad. Actually, he responded better than she'd expected. After lunch, she decided not to even go back to the office. Since she was already downtown she decided to do some shopping. She would definitely need at least two new bathing suits. Her figure was still intact at a size 12, and her curves were in all the right places. She still turned many heads— just not John's. He hardly noticed she was alive except for work.

After shopping she went straight home and started packing. She called Patty and her mom to let them know that she was ready and would drop the kids off on tomorrow night. Their flight was scheduled to leave at six Friday morning. After ten years, she had only taken one vacation, and that was to attend John's grand- mother's funeral in Atlanta. She deserved this long-overdue time to herself, and she was looking forward to every minute of it.

With Hope and the kids gone, John was looking forward to having the house to himself and just relaxing. However, destiny had another plan. He was annoyed about the phone call he received early that morning. Now he was on his way to meet with some guy named Peter Hampton who said he had some photos and information that he was sure John would be interested in.

Shit! John thought. He immediately thought about his fre- quent visits to the park and the bathroom. So when this Peter Hampton said to meet him at 10:00 a.m. at Starbucks, he quickly agreed.

John arrived at Starbucks and realized he didn't even know what Peter Hampton looked like.

"Good morning, Mr. Darroff," a short balding man said.

"You must be Peter Hampton. Good morning," said John as he sat at the table. "Let's cut to the chase, Mr. Hampton. What is it that you feel I *need* to know?"

Peter pulled out a manila envelope and handed it to John. The envelope was filled with pictures of John's frequent trips to the bathroom at Hess and pictures of him at the park with various men. Nothing incriminating, just pictures of him in those secret rendezvous spots.

"Okay? So why are you going around taking pictures of me?" "Your wife hired me. She thinks you're having an affair with some other woman. When I realized that you were the husband, I knew from the start that she was wrong. You see, Mr. Darroff, I've seen you myself in various places where men seek men for all kinds of sexual pleasures. I know who you are. You're a very popular visitor. I thought it would only be fair that I tell you about your wife's suspicions and of my role as her hired investigator. Now, I could have just continued following you and could have gotten some more explicit pictures, but since we're a part of the same team, I wanted to give you an opportunity to tell me how you want me to proceed."

John was flabbergasted. This one had caught him off guard. As thoughts ran through his mind, one of those thoughts was if Hope was trying to find evidence to use in divorce proceedings. All this time he thought he had the upper hand over Hope. He never thought she'd go this far. He never thought she'd divorce him. He thought she was such a family-oriented person and loved the image of family life. But she had stepped out of her comfort zone and actually hired an investigator. Initially he was pissed, but after further thought, he was relieved destiny had led her to this Peter Hampton guy. Anyone else would have found out the truth and shared it with her. She would definitely have grounds for a divorce and then possibly take everything in the proceed- ings. Now, he had to find out just what Peter wanted from him.

All John could say is "well damn" as he shook his head. "Well, I'm glad you called and shared this information with me, Peter. So, she thinks I'm having an affair…with another woman. We both know that's not true." He chuckled. "So, tell me, what do you plan to do with these photos?"

"I'll sell these and the negative to you. I can take photos of you just going about your daily business life and tell Mrs. Darroff that I found no evidence of you having any affair. But that's gonna cost you some money."

"Hmm. Okay. How much we talkin'?" "Ten grand"

"Ten grand!

"It'll cost you a lot more than that if your wife gets a hold of the real deal about you, Mr. Darroff. I think ten grand is a bargain considering your business, house—your total net worth!"

John thought about it. If he paid this guy the ten grand, how could he be sure that he wouldn't come back later asking for another ten grand?

"Okay. I need about a month to get that much together. How do I know you won't come back later asking for more money though?"

Peter chuckled and replied, "You don't." And just like that, John was like a deer caught in headlights of a car; he didn't know if the car would hit him or if it would swerve away—and Peter was the driver.

Hope didn't realize just how exhausted she was. She passed up hanging out at the club last night. Instead she found comfort in the oversized bed with fluffy pillows and fell asleep. She didn't wake up until noon the next day. Patty had left a note saying she'd be on the beach. Hope showered, put on her bathing suit, and went down to the resort's beachfront to look for Patty. She saw her talking with a handsome man. The man looked familiar, but Hope couldn't place where she'd seen him.

"Good morning, sleeping beauty," Patty greeted her with a smile and a hug. "You must have really been tired. You missed all the fun last night! This is Ray. He's from Philly too. He was actually on the same flight we were on. Ray, this is my cousin, Hope."

"It's a pleasure to meet you," he said while extending his hand. Hope shook his hand and replied, "Yes, it's a pleasure meeting you as well." She looked over at Patty with a puzzled look on her face as her stomach started to rumble.

Ray heard it too. "Well, it's about time for some lunch. Would you, ladies, care to join me for lunch?"

Patty declined, stating that she was still full from breakfast at the hotel's breakfast buffet. Hope was famished and immediately took Ray up on his offer.

Ray was an interesting character. He was into real estate development. He was divorced from his wife for five years and had a younger girlfriend whom he was getting tired of. He sat on the board of the Boys and Girls Club, did a lot of work in the community, and he was fine as hell. His voice was so smooth that Hope complimented him by telling him he should be a DJ. They spent the day on the beach together talking, laughing, and sip- ping Bahama Mamas. He was good company for her especially since Patty had gone off with the owner of the club she met last night. She ended up having dinner with Ray later that evening. He was such a gentleman, something she was missing in her life. It was refreshing to have stimulating conversation with a man who was sincerely interested in her thoughts and opinions.

After dinner and dancing, he walked her to her room and kissed her hand good night. It was a soft kiss that made her rem-

inisce about John the night Kennedy was conceived. A simple thing like this was all she desired from John but did not receive it. She longed for someone to truly caress her loneliness. Ray's soft kiss had brought back all these feelings that she missed. This was the perfect time to invite him inside her room to finish what- ever he was thinking when he placed a kiss on her hand. But she remembered her vows and quickly came to her senses. She didn't even realize it was 3:00 a.m. as she bid Ray good night.

Patty had not returned to the room, which Hope found out after she stepped inside and leaned her back against the door thinking about the opportunity she just gave up. Frustrated, she took a cold shower to calm her hormones and went right to sleep.

She was awakened by the sound of Patty coming in and the door slamming closed. "Sorry, cuz. I didn't mean to wake you. But since you're awake now, you might as well get up and get dressed. Jeff invited us to go out on his glass bottom boat for the day!"

Patty always had that effect on men. They just seemed to clamor toward her and want to shower her with expensive mate- rial things. She and Hope were the same age but lived quite dif- ferent lives. Patty had never been married but had a career as a computer analyst at a major IT firm. She started there as a sec- retary twenty years ago, took classes at night, earned her master's degree, and had worked her way up to senior management. She traveled a lot for work and lived in a penthouse on the waterfront.

Yes, cousin Patty was no stranger to the finer things in life and had always been good to Hope and her kids. She never cared for John at all and made no secret about how she felt. But she under- stood why Hope loved him. He first represented himself as a man of God. He attended church regularly, and that was what Hope loved most about him. They would have Bible study together and were always at some church function. Patty just never liked him. He seemed pretentious like there was something fake about him. He was loud, obnoxious, and overbearing behind closed

doors. She heard him belittling her cousin about her clothes. She watched Hope transform her style from fly girl to homey. John hadn't changed a thing—except Hope. He was still a flashy dresser, and he was a flirt. Always up in some woman's face. Patty hated him to the second power.

After they were married, Hope stopped hanging out with her friends and rarely attended family functions anymore. Her chil- dren barely knew their side of the family, but they knew all of John's family—from Atlanta to Boston. As far as Patty was con- cerned, her cousin deserved better. She felt this guy Ray would be good for her. They had extensive conversations their first night on the island and the following morning. He made no secret that he was interested in Hope and not her. She liked that. So she felt him out. Learned that he was a residential real estate devel- oper and also owned a popular banquet hall in the city. He was divorced, and yes, he had a girlfriend, but she was not with him on this trip, and that was all that mattered.

"How was your lunch with Ray? Girl that man is *phine*! I saw him looking at me and then looking around. Girl, he was looking for you. He said he spotted you on the plane, and when he saw me, he knew you were close, but you never showed up. So, do you like him?"

"Yes, he was very nice. We had a good time I almost invited him in the room, if you know what I mean," Hope replied as she made her way to the bathroom to shower.

"Good. I just saw him and invited him to spend the day with us." Even though Hope was already in the bathroom, Patty felt the smile that was on Hope's face and heart. Knowing that Hope was still smiling, she shouted, "You're welcome, girl."

Back at home, John was smiling too. John was excited that Mr. Strong invited him to play golf the next morning. Adam picked John up at 5:30 a.m. He told John about some of the people they'd be playing golf with today: the mayor, the governor, owners of some the largest construction management firms in the city as well as developers and major-league athletes. All the time they were riding, John kept thinking that Adam seemed familiar but he couldn't put his finger on it. When they arrived, Adam introduced him to the others, as they formed teams and then proceeded to play 18 holes. By the end of the game, he had been invited to the mayor's birthday party the following Saturday and to the governor's ball in two weeks! He was ecstatic. Still, he couldn't place his finger on where he had seen Adam Strong before. Then he saw some eye contact between Adam and one of the caddies.

Nah, John thought. *Can't be.* Then John's mind traveled to some of the places he had recently visited. It was then that John remembered where he'd seen Adam—in the men's room at Hess.

Adam and John were both silent during the first ten minutes of their hour-long ride home. Each man was deep inside his own thoughts. Adam finally broke the silence.

"So, I see you like to play with boys too, huh?"

John looked him in the eye and replied, "You have something in your eye. Want me to blow it for you?"

They both laughed. "I thought you looked familiar, and I thought I caught a glimpse of a twinkle in your eye, but I wasn't sure."

"Well, you'll have no problem fitting in with the good ole boys. No problem at all."

"Well, I do have this one problem," John replied. "My wife has hired some private dick to follow me. She thinks I'm having an affair with my secretary. This guy called me up the other day.

Seems he knows all the rendezvous spots and has seen me out and about. He's blackmailing me for ten grand! And I'm sure he'll come back later for more money. I can't allow my wife to find out about my lifestyle. She'll divorce me and take everything."

"This private dick. His name wouldn't be Peter Hampton, would it?" Adam asked.

"Yeah. That's his name. You know him?" John asked.

"You don't have to worry about him much longer. He's gotten greedy, and now he's threatening some real top-notch bigwigs. I understand his days are numbered. You don't have to worry about that."

"So, your wife has no clue about your lifestyle? She such a sweet and gorgeous woman. She's funny and intelligent too. I love her spirit. She gives you the perfect image. Use it to your advantage. She's very charming, and no matter what, the good ole boys still love a charming woman. Just her presence will take you and your company a long way, John. You're gonna have to be extra kind to her. Show her love, and if she ever finds out, it won't be as bad as you think. Not if you treat her right. Right now she doesn't look very happy. And taking a vacation in the Bahamas without you shows that she needed to get away from you. Young man, you gotta treat your woman right. You gotta treat her like a queen. If you do, then I can guarantee that she'll forgive you for many things. Believe me. I know."

Brenda was a cheerleader and often traveled with the football team. She wasn't interested in any of the players but could have had any of them. They were either womanizers, gays, or just overly arrogant assholes. She'd heard rumors that most of them were bisexual and had women on the side. With the AIDS statistics rising on campus, she was inclined to believe the rumors. She

wanted no part of any football player. She spotted Adam their second year in college. He was captain of the track team and was built like an Adonis. Brenda tried to get his attention in the classes they had together, but that didn't work. Then she started hanging out at the track, and that didn't work either. When she found out that he and his roommate Doug hung out at the local restaurant and grill, she began hanging out there too hoping to catch his eye. After their second year in college she decided to make the first move.

One day after class she walked up to him and introduced her- self. He said he knew who she was. She offered to take him to dinner on the spot. He seemed kinda shy but accepted on the condition that he pays. He was always a leader and intent on being successful. He was different from the other boys in college. He actually respected her mind, thoughts, and opinions. His first priority wasn't sex. In fact, if she hadn't made the initial move toward sex, it may have never happened. He was so inexperienced that she thought he was a virgin, but she never asked. The time they spent together was far more fulfilling than their sex life. He was such an adventurer. Before graduating he was offered a posi- tion as a project manager at McGraw Hill, and he asked her to marry him, and she gladly accepted. She was sure the sex would get better with time.

It was a small, beautiful intimate ceremony, just Adam's younger brother John as best man and Brenda's sister Karen was matron of honor. It had puzzled Brenda that his best friend and room- mate Doug did not want to be a part of the wedding. They were inseparable in school. Not only were they roommates, but they were also buddies and were together most of the time. Not only was he not in the wedding, but he also didn't even come. Adam said he was out of the country. Not many of Adam's friends came to the wedding. Not even his best friend from childhood that he always spoke of so fondly. Just a few of his frat brothers and his

family. Brenda's family and close friends were also in attendance. It was a beautiful occasion and the best day of Brenda's life.

They went to Jamaica for their honeymoon, and Brenda couldn't wait until they made love. They only made love three times in two years. The first time Adam was very nervous and a little clumsy. But once he got started it was amazing. He flipped her and took her from the back all three times, and she liked it. When she asked why he didn't want to make love more often, Adam said he really wanted to wait until they were married. When he fell asleep on the wedding night without laying so much as an eye on her, she was deeply disappointed but under- stood that he was probably just extremely tired.

When she woke up the next morning, Adam had ordered breakfast and fed her in bed. Then he told her to shower, dress, and meet him in the lobby because he had an entire day planned for them. He was so thoughtful. When she got to the lobby, she spotted Adam talking with a man who suddenly vanished when she walked up.

"Hi, honey. I'm ready. Who was that you were talking to?" "Oh, hey babe. You look stunning. Come, your chariot awaits."

He dismissed her question about the man he was talking to, and she didn't think twice about it once she saw the long stretch limo waiting for them outside.

The limo drove them to a Rockhouse Hotel Restaurant over- looking the beautiful beach of Negril. They had lunch there and then enjoyed a couple's day at the spa. He surprised her with a suite there for the night, and they ate dinner on the balcony under the moonlit sky. Afterward they went down to the lounge and danced the night away while drinking never-ending glasses of Jamaican kiss drinks. By the time they got back to their suite, Brenda was so drunk she passed out as soon as she lay down.

The next day the limo drove them to Ocho Rios where they explored the Green Grotto Caves. They learned about the history of the place as a haven for runaway slaves, and the small lake's water was crystal clear.

During dinner Adam received a page and excused himself to go find a phone. By the time he returned Brenda had finished her dinner, and Adam seemed a bit nervous.

"Honey, I'm sorry. We have to cut our honeymoon short. We'll have to leave tomorrow morning. I have to get back to work early. There's been an accident on one of the job sites."

The drive back to the hotel was four hours long, and once they got to the room it was a little past midnight. Adam spent the evening finding a flight out of Jamaica to Philadelphia the next morning. He booked them on a 6:00 a.m. flight, which meant they needed to be at the airport by 4:00 a.m. They spent the rest of the time packing. They barely spoke. Brenda was quiet because she didn't want to show how disappointed she was about the honeymoon being cut short. She understood Adam had just started this job, and if he had to get back, then so be it. She would support him in everything he did and would not question his decisions. She was determined to be a good wife and make their home a loving place where he would be happy to come to after a hard day's work. Then it dawned on her: They hadn't even con- summated their marriage! Now she wanted to cry. But she didn't. She just continued packing in silence.

Adam's thoughts were totally someplace else. The page was not from his job. It was from Doug.

Adam had always had sexual feeling toward males. His first encounter happened when he was ten years old. His best buddy from down the street named Danny was his first. Danny was older than Adam and always let him tag along behind him throughout the neighborhood. Everybody in the neighborhood knew Danny, so Adam felt honored to be his friend. Danny's mom was a great cook, and Adam often ate dinner there. One night they had been watching movies, and it got late, so Danny asked his mom if Adam could spend the night. Adam called his mom, and she said it was okay. That night they lay in bed talking and laughing, and before they knew it, they were kissing. They were inseparable after that night, but they were always very careful to not let their secret relationship known to the other guys. They continued their secret relationship until Adam went off to college.

Doug and Adam met during freshmen year in college. They were roommates from two different sides of the track. Adam was there on full scholarship, and Doug's family was rich and paid cash for his tuition. They became best friends, and eventu- ally they became lovers. By junior year, Doug had become much more effeminate in his appearance, speech, and actions. He didn't care what people thought. He had that luxury. Adam didn't. He couldn't afford to jeopardize his scholarship in any way, and if his teammates found out his secret, they would surely ostracize him. With the way they talked about homos in the locker room, it was clear that they did not approve of that lifestyle.

During senior year Adam told Doug that he was dating Brenda, and Doug threw a sissy fit. Adam tried to make Doug understand his situation. Adam knew that being openly gay would disappoint his family and possibly hurt his chances at get- ting a job with a Fortune 500 company, which had been his life- long goal. He had a responsibility to his family, his community, and his race to live a "normal" lifestyle, which included getting married and having a family. It was hard enough being a black man; he didn't want the extra burden of being gay too.

Doug, being the spoiled rich kid, could not see things from Adam's point of view. He didn't care who knew he was gay. His family was filthy rich. He came from a long line of politicians, judges, and attorneys from his maternal and paternal sides. There

were gays and lesbians in his family, and they still earned above- average wages because they could always work for the family law firm or get a job using his family's connections; gay or not, his life wouldn't be altered in any way. Still they continued their relation- ship in secrecy, but Adam continued dating Brenda.

After graduation they rarely saw each other, but when Adam told Doug they were getting married, Doug actually broke down and cried. "You told me you loved me, Adam. What am I sup- posed to do?"

"Come to my wedding and wish me happiness," Adam replied. Doug hung up on him, and they didn't speak any more until Adam got his page this evening. Doug had gone to Paris and had just returned. He missed Adam and wanted to see him. Adam missed him too and couldn't wait to see him again. He couldn't even make love to his new wife because his mind was on Doug. He knew that soon he would run out of excuses and would have to make love to his new wife. She had to be thinking something was wrong. His excuse about being called back to work would carry him for a few additional days, he thought. Maybe seeing Doug would help him to get his head straight.

Brenda was happy being married to Adam. Their sex life had even gotten better. He always liked to do it from the back and doggie style, and she was fine with that. She actually enjoyed this aggressive side of him.

In just a few years Adam was promoted to vice president of McGraw Cooper, and they were a dashing power couple. They were now socialites and attended lots of prestigious gatherings in Philadelphia and New York. He showered her with lavish gifts of fine jewelry and furs. Life was good. But after their second daughter Naila was born, she began noticing odd behavior patterns. Adam always seemed to catch the eyes of strange men when they were out. Men would actually come up to him and compliment him on his tie or his suit. There were lots of signs, and she ignored them all. He was a good husband, father, and provider, and that was all that mattered to her. But one day an incident happened that she could not ignore.

It was Father's Day. Brenda was getting the girls ready to go to Karen's house for their annual Father's Day cookout. Karen's husband, Jack, loved to grill and did his thing every Father's Day. Adam told Karen he was going to run by Doug's house and would be right back. Karen bathed the girls, dressed them, and braided their hair. Two hours went by, and Adam hadn't returned home nor had he answered her many text messages. When he finally came home, she asked him where he had been. He told her he was with Doug.

"Well, what were you doing that you couldn't answer my pages or even call?"

Adam said, "We were just talking." "About what?"

"Sex."

"What about it!" Brenda asked.

Adam was against a wall. He had to be honest with Brenda. She deserved the truth, but he didn't want to hurt her.

"Baby. Sit down for a minute."

"No, Adam, we don't have time for this right now. We're late for the cookout. We can talk about this later. Come on, girls. Time to go."

Later that night after they put the girls to bed, Adam came clean and told Brenda the whole truth. Brenda was devastated and began vomiting. Adam rubbed her back and dried her tears as she cried for about twenty minutes straight. She was numb.

She couldn't believe it. She who had been so careful not to fall for any gay down-low football players on campus, she who knew all the signs of a down-low man was now confronted with the fact that she was actually married to one? As the past flashed before her, she realized that all the signs were there—she just didn't see them. Or she just didn't want to see them. She didn't want to know the truth. How else could she explain her stupidity? *All the signs were there staring her right in the face, and she ignored them.*

She didn't want it to be true. Her fairy tale lifestyle was all just a lie. She was devastated. But she would not let this destroy her family; her children would have a normal life even if she had to live a lie. She still loved her husband even though he told her, and he understood if she wanted a divorce. But she didn't want that. She wanted her family to stay together. So she made the decision to stay and deal with it. As long as he didn't throw his lifestyle in her face and respected her, she thought she could deal with it. She continued to be a dutiful wife and played her part, planning din- ner parties for his business associates and their wives. She soon learned that she wasn't the only wife in this situation. The higher Adam climbed that corporate ladder, and the more they became a part of the lifestyle of the rich and famous, the more debauchery. She soon stopped attending parties and focused on her home and her children. Yes, she still loved Adam very much, but she made him use a condom whenever they had any type of sexual contact.

As the years went by and their children got older, Brenda became bitter and angry about her life. For years she had kept up appearances just to make Adam look good in front of busi- ness partners and prospects, but now she wanted more. So she made Adam finance her PR and marketing firm and also made sure that he directed business in her direction. Soon she was a millionaire in her own right—independent of Adam. She had her own money and prestige. She had maintained her sanity and dignity, but she was still very bitter, and nobody messed with her.

They respected her, but she had no real friends because she was a mean, bitter, and angry woman. No one ever really understood why because she never shared her story.

Hope couldn't believe how fast four days flew by. She spent the last night walking on the beach with Ray, and they stayed up all night talking. They watched the beautiful sunrise over the ocean, which helped set the mood as he kissed her ever so gently on the tip of her luscious lips. Then he took her gently by the hand and walked her back to her hotel. They exchanged numbers and promised to stay in contact. Now here she was in Patty's BMW trying to hold on to those memorable moments spent with Ray as she headed back to her dreaded reality. She eagerly wondered if Mr. Hampton had anything to report, as this would be the perfect time to get any evidence to file for a divorce. Ray showed her how she was supposed to be treated. She immediately checked her voicemail messages, and there weren't any messages from him. Now she was getting a little suspicious. It had been a month since they met. Surely he should have something. She made a mental note to call him first thing in the morning.

John had picked the kids up from her mom's house, and they were all anxiously waiting for her to walk through the door.

"Moommyyy!" The girls screamed in unison as then ran and smothered her with hugs and kisses.

Even John seemed happy to see her. "Hey, honey. Did you have a good time?" he asked as he kissed her. "You look good. Relaxed. Let me take your bags upstairs."

What the what! Hope was shocked. She couldn't remember the last time John said two nice words to her. Now here he was actually talking in sentences nicely? Plus kissing her! She knew something was up. *Maybe he found out about Peter Hampton*, she thought. *Maybe he got a nice big contract.* She was uneasy about that whole scene that had just taken place.

She stayed up talking and playing with the girls for about two more hours as a pleasant way of avoiding John. When she finally put them to bed, John was already asleep. Hope used that time to call her mom. She was hoping that her mom could fill her in on anything that John had said while picking up the kids.

Her mom brought her up to date on all the family gossip, but most of all she was excited about her upcoming retirement party. Her son, Donté, had called. Hope barely remembered her brother. He was ten years older and had gone to live with his father in Boston when he was thirteen and Hope was two. He went to live with his father shortly after Hope's father died. Donté had visited one summer when Hope was five years old. After that, she never saw him again. Mom always acted like it was such a big deal whenever she heard from Donté. She never talked about Hope's father or why Donté went to live in Boston with his dad, but she always raved about what a good boy Donté was. Hope hardly remembered any of it; she hardly knew her brother, but for some reason, just the mention of his name gave her chills. But she let her mom go on about how wonderful and successful her son was doing and how he was actually coming to her retirement party. Hope told her mom she was happy and looked forward to seeing Donté. Deep down she had that queasy feeling she always got anytime anyone mentioned Donté. She tried to sneak in ques- tions that could get her more insight why John was acting so nice, but her mom was caught up in her moment with Donté. Hope said good-bye to her mom, strolled back in the room, and called it a night.

Hope overslept. She woke up to a house that was silent and empty. John had left a note on the kitchen table telling her that he'd see her at the office when she got there. Breakfast was laid out on the table, though John ordered in. But at least he made time to take it out the bag and romantically spread it on the table. The note also said he didn't want to disturb her sleep because she looked so peaceful. He even drew a heart under his signature. She began to wonder who this stranger was and why did he choose to appear when Ray was now in the picture of her mind. John always woke her up to get the kids ready for school no matter how tired she had been. He would drive them to school, but it was up to Hope to get them up, dress them, and make breakfast and lunches for them. She was puzzled that all of these things were done, but she enjoyed the peaceful moments and took her time getting ready to go to the office.

When she arrived at the office, she learned why John had been in such a good mood. In just a few days, they received two major electrical contracts: one for the new convention center and one for the new stadium. And these weren't subcontracts either; these were major big contracts straight from the construction man- agement firm of Strong Industries. The contracts were on her desk waiting for her signature. The two contracts totaled 15.5 *million* dollars. She wondered who did the projections and what the profit would be. John interrupted her thoughts as he entered the office.

"Welcome back, baby! Can you believe it? Fifteen million dol- lars for just two contracts! Adam took me out to play golf this weekend, and I met a lot of people baby. This is just the beginning!"

"This is unbelievable!" Hope replied. "How did you come up with the projections so fast? Did someone check the num- bers? What's the profit margin? Did you sign a contract with the Electrician Union? You know we have to use union workers in Philly. Did—"

"Damn it!" He leaped over and jumped in her face. "Just *sign*
the contract, Hope! So my company can get started."

Now, that's the John I know. I was wondering who that stran- ger was last night, and this morning. I knew it wouldn't last. "Your company? I own 51 percent, remember? So I have a stake in eve- rything that goes on in this company, John. All I'm doing is try- ing to make sure that we can do the job without losing money. It's not like that hasn't happened before."

"Oh, here we go. You throwing my mistakes back up in my face again. You ain't never satisfied. So what if we lost money? Have you ever missed a meal? Huh? Have you ever been evicted? Huh?" Then he grabbed her by the neck and began to choke her.

"Bitch, just sign the damn contract! Asking me all these damn questions. I know what I'm doing, okay? All I need you to do is sign the contract so we can get paid, okay! And don't ask me no more questions about *my* company!"

He finally let go of her neck as she dropped to the floor gasp- ing for air. John put a pen on the table and said, "Now. Sign it."

She crawled over to the desk, pulled herself up, took the pen, and signed the contract. John snatched the papers up and strolled toward the door. Before opening the door to leave, he turned to her and said, "Get up and get yourself together before you come out of this office."

Then John thought about what Adam said. *She gives you the perfect image. Use it to your advantage. She's very charming, and the good ole boys still love a charming woman like Hope. Just her presence will take you and your company a long way, John. You're gonna have to be extra kind to her.*

"Listen, Hope. I'm sorry. You can recheck the numbers. Any changes to the scope of work will be added and charged as extra work orders. Adam's project manager helped me with the bid. But you worry too much, baby. I know things have been bad in the past, but that's all behind us now. I'm in with the right people, and things are looking up. Trust me on this okay?"

Hope stared at him in disbelief.

"Now, take the day off, go get your hair done, and get a mani- cure and pedicure." He walked over and gently took her hand in his. "We have a fund-raiser to attend tonight. Tomorrow we have to attend a ball at the governor's mansion, and Saturday we've been invited to spend the day on Adam's boat with his family."

Hope looked in his face and was petrified. She watched him turn from an angry wolf to a loving lamb in less than sixty sec- onds. She decided to play along because she didn't know what he was capable of.

"Um. Okay," she finally managed to say. "I'm sorry. This is all just so sudden. I mean, I was gone for four days, came back, and my whole world has done a complete 180."

"That's right, baby. Just enjoy it. You've worked so hard for so long; now it's time to enjoy the fruits of your labor. You don't even need to come into the office every day if you don't want to. All you have to do is be my wife and help me shine."

He kissed her on the forehead and left. Hope sat there in a state of shock and confusion. She finally pulled out her com- pact and fixed her face and hair. She looked at her neck and saw whelps were beginning to form where his fingers tightly gripped it. *I'll be sure to get an updo for tonight so everyone can see these bruises on my neck*, she thought. Then she got up and walked down the hallways, smiled, and nodded to the employees who spoke as she passed by. She couldn't get out of there fast enough. She didn't know how much longer she could wear this thick mask that was fading thin.

Help him shine! Hope replayed John's words in her mind as she walked down Broad Street. *That's all I've ever done. But you know what? I'm gonna do exactly what he said—just enjoy the ride while it lasts*, she thought. She stopped at a newsstand to pick up the latest edition of *Vogue* to look through while at the hair salon. As

she reached for the magazine, she glanced at the headline on the daily newspaper: Local Private Detective Found Shot In Center City.

"Oh my god!" She flipped to page 3 to read the story. It was Peter Hampton! She remembered her mental note to call him, but unfortunately it had slipped her mind because of the new John found when she got home. The article said he was found dead in his office yesterday with a single bullet wound to the head. There were no witnesses and no suspects. *Sounds like he was executed*, she thought. How strange that it happened right when she was having him investigate John. She wondered if John found out and killed him. Ordinarily she would have laughed at that thought, but after that episode in her office just minutes ago, she wouldn't put anything past John. *Someone* was angry enough to kill him.

Poor man. God rest his soul. She couldn't help wondering if he'd found anything out about John. If John had found out that she hired him and killed him—or had him killed. She was very afraid and decided at that moment to just go along with whatever John said. She began to pray right then and there. She would leave everything in God's hands. He would handle it. She knew the plans God had for her. Plans for her to be happy and prosper- ous. Not plans for hurt and despair. She would let her husband lead, and she would follow, just as the church instructed.

The next few years went by without incident between John and Hope. But Hope never let her guard down, knowing that the real John Darroff could appear at any moment. Those three years went by quickly. They was a whirlwind of parties, balls, fund-raisers, and trips. Literally, that is all Hope did for the past three years. No work. She didn't even go into the office for meetings. All the business deals now took place at the balls, fund-raisers, and

parties they attended. The attendees included politicians, judges, lawyers, and bankers. She had no idea that there was always a secret room at these parties, and John and most of the other men always seemed to disappear for about an hour or so. John told her they had a private room to make private deals. She would be busy chatting with the other ladies and a few men

When she wasn't attending parties, she spent a lot of time volunteering at the church, feeding the homeless, and working with the youth groups that her children were involved with, even though they were full grown teens now. Kamari was sixteen, and Kennedy was eighteen, getting ready to graduate high school and on her way to Taubman College in the fall. Hope was happy to be able to bond with her over the past year. Life was great. There were no shutoff notices, all the bills were being paid, there was money in the bank accounts, and she was living the life of a wife and mother—just as she'd always dreamed of. She completely forgot about Ray. After all those years of praying, God had finally answered her prayers. She knew he would. She praised him con- tinually for turning her life around in just a short amount of time. She knew nothing was too hard for God! She met lots of people at the events they attended, most of whom she had only read about in newspapers and magazines. She was now part of the in crowd. It was nothing for her to have tea with the wives of may- ors and governors. She'd have lunch at prestigious country clubs with the wives of developers and big businessmen. Her children attended schools with the elite, and these were now their play- mates. Hope often took her mother with her wherever she went now that her mom was retired; they spent a great amount of time together. Hope enjoyed the quality time with her mom.

Her mom was really disappointed when Donté didn't show up for her retirement party, and Hope vowed to never allow that look of disappointment to come across her mother's face again. They had become best friends. Bernie never felt quite comfort-

able in their new circle. She often complained that they gave her the creeps and that there was something about that Adam Strong; she just couldn't put her finger on.

Of all the people that Hope met in this new circle, oddly enough she found herself closest to the one that all the other wives called the Big Bad Bitch. Mrs. Adam Strong a.k.a. Brenda Strong. Yes, she was a pistol, but for some reason she was very kind to Hope. They spent spa days together, and she invited Hope to accompany her on business trips to Italy and Paris. Brenda was tall and very beautiful. She could have easily been a model. She was very fashion conscious and helped Hope with her new image. When they first met at the mayor's birthday party, Brenda was very standoffish and cold toward Hope.

One Sunday afternoon when they were all at Adam's house for a BBQ, Brenda told Hope that her image was all wrong. "You look too homey. You have pretty skin, teeth, and hair, but you don't know how to flaunt them. Here, take this card and call my image consultant first thing tomorrow morning."

Of course Hope's pride prevented her from accepting the card;
the next day she received a call from André himself.

"Hello, I'm looking for Mrs. Hope Darroff." "This is her
speaking."

"Mrs. Darroff, I was instructed to give you a call to schedule an appointment. I will be at your house today at 3:00 p.m. See you then." And he hung up.

She didn't even give him her address or confirmed that she wanted his services. She was furious now! Who did Mrs. Brenda Strong think she was? First telling her that her image was wrong, then giving her phone number and address to a complete stran- ger who sounded like a rainbow of skittles. How else would this André know where she lived? She had a good mind to call him back and tell him not to come, but instead asked the helper to

prepare tea and sandwiches for 3:00 p.m. She spent the rest of the morning and early afternoon trying to look presentable. She decided to pin her hair up, applied a small amount of make-up for a natural look, and selected a tan wrap dress and pumps. She wore a single strand of pearls around her neck, a pearl bracelet, and earrings. When she was finally finished, she looked in the mirror and was pleased.

"Now let's see what Mr. Image Consultant has to say. I look good!"

The doorbell rang, and she allowed Hazel to answer it. She showed André to the backyard where she had tea and sandwiches ready. Hope wanted to make an impressive entrance. When she came out the door, André looked at her and laughed.

"Honey, you ain't June Cleaver, and this ain't *Father Knows Best*!" And he started laughing hysterically. Whew! Honey, I needed that laugh. When Brenda told me you needed a little help, that was an understatement. Where did you get that outfit? Lord and Taylor?" André sure was handsome but obviously gay.

"Yes, I did. What's wrong with my outfit? This is how the ladies at the club all dress for tea in the afternoon. I thought this outfit would be appropriate." Hope was insulted by André's remarks.

"Honey, that's fine for them. But you ain't them. You have to be you and have your own style." He began pulling the hair- pins out of her hair. "Look at this head full of luscious thick hair. Girlfriend, you need some highlights and a cut to give your hair some shape," he explained as he ruffled and tossed her hair around.

"Walk over there and turn around so I can see your shape." Hope obeyed.

"Umm hmm. Nice little hourglass shape, a little hippy but still a cute shape. Nice legs too. Okay. Let me see your closet."

Hope quietly led him upstairs to her walk-in closet. "Girl, you are so drab! Almost everything in here is gray, white, black-and- white. And black makes gray. So, honey, you're gray. Do you know what gray symbolizes? Boring, drab, depressing. Okay. Let's go." Hope didn't ask any questions. She just followed André out- side and got in the passenger side of his red Porsche and rode in silence.

"First, we're going to Panaché to get that hair shaped and highlighted. Then we'll hit a couple of boutiques downtown and start creating a look that is all yours. Your own signature style. A woman in your position needs to have a style that identifies her and her alone. Look at Brenda. That woman is fierce! She was already fierce when she came to me, I just added a few touches, but she was already doing most of her shopping in Milan and Paris."

He went on and on about Brenda. Hope thought she always looked nice but didn't know her outfits came from Milan and Paris. Well, maybe she did need a makeover. So she just sat back and let André lead the way. She got her hair and make-up done and ended up spending $250 on make-up and an instruc- tional video.

To help her create different looks, they went to South Street and spent hours shopping. André started with accessories. "At least you can accessorize and dress up some of those pieces in that drab closet at home. Most of that stuff needs to go in the trash or to the Salvation Army. I did see a few pieces that we can salvage and dress up with the right accessories."

They had bags full of shoes, handbags, earrings, necklaces, bracelets, belts, and a few exquisite-looking rings. Then André picked out some dresses. He picked up a hot-pink plain sheath and a multicolored maxi dress that looked kind of kaleidoscope- ish to Hope. He insisted that this was one of the latest fashions for the season and that Hope should wear it to an afternoon out- ing. He picked out a sexy red dress, a white one, a royal blue one,

and a mint-green one. They mostly argued about the clothing that André picked out, but in the end she purchased everything he chose for her. She knew this new look would take some get- ting used to. And what would John think?

"Honey if he's anything like the men I know, he's gonna love it! Trust!" André assured Hope.

When John came home that night it was late, but Hope pur- posely waited up for him to see what he thought of her new look. She put on a silk lingerie, robe set, and tightened up her make-up and hair. He came in, apologized for being late, kissed her on the forehead, and went to bed. He never even noticed. He had been so busy lately he hardly saw her or the girls. When he did see them in the mornings, he was rushing and preoccupied. The girls were becoming resentful, as they wondered why Daddy was hardly ever home even on the weekends. They spent a lot of time with Hope's mom because most weekends she and John attended some type of event somewhere. They loved staying a G'mom's house, and G'mom loved having them. But still, they missed their daddy.

The next day she decided to surprise John at work. She didn't want to give him too big of a shock, so she put on one of her old tan dresses with some new accessories, did her make-up and hair, put on a pair of black-and-tan ankle-strap wedge heels, and strutted into the office. She was feeling like her old self—sexy and confident—and it showed.

When she walked in the office she was shocked at the renova- tions that had taken place. The reception area was entirely new with a new sign that read "J. D. Industries LLC." An entirely new company. All the offices were remodeled, and the whole layout was completely different. The receptionist didn't even know who she was.

"Good afternoon. May I help you?" she asked politely. She was a cute young girl and was professional and dressed appropriately.

"Um, yes. Mrs. Darroff here to see my husband," Hope stuttered. "Oh, hello, Mrs.

Darroff. It's nice to meet you. One moment
please, I believe they're still in a meeting." She buzzed the phone
and told someone that Mrs. Darroff was here to see her husband.

"He'll be right out, ma'am."

Hope walked around the lobby area admiring the art and the decor. It looked really nice. Just then John came out to the lobby. "Hey, honey! What a surprise! Come on back, let me show you what's been going on."

He took her back, and she saw that the renovations were still taking place. They had knocked down walls and built up walls, expanded some offices especially his and condensed others— including hers. "Well, since you're not here on a daily basis, we felt you didn't need a large office space."

"Who is 'we'?" Hope wanted to know.

"We have some new business partners: Brad Anderson from Anderson

Construction Company and real estate developer Fred Neilson. They'll both be here in about fifteen minutes, so you'll get a chance to meet them."

He still hadn't said anything about her new look, and Hope forgot about it herself for a moment.

"Why wasn't I informed about all these changes taking place, John? How come I wasn't involved in the decision-making pro- cess? If I'm not going to be a part of the decisions, I want my name taken off as part owner of the company. I can't have my name involved when things are taking place that I'm not aware of. This—"

"No problem, Hope. As you may have noticed the company has changed its name and with it the officers. You are not an officer of

J. D. Industries LLC. You are an officer of J. D. & Associates Inc. Two completely different companies, my dear. The only contracts going on with your company are the convention center and the stadium. All the larger contracts are under J. D. Industries LLC."

Hope was stunned.

"By the way, I love your new look. You are stunning. Come. Lunch is in the conference room. Brad and Fred will be here any minute."

When she entered the conference room it was decked out with an oval-shaped cherrywood table and burgundy leather chairs. The draperies were green, gold, and burgundy; and the carpet was green. There was a buffet table on one wall that was filled with food: roast beef and gravy, potatoes, turkey, stuffing, string beans, greens, a large bowl of fruit salad, and a tray of veggies. There was a variety of bottled drinks and water. The plates, napkins, and flatware all matched the decor of the room.

"Well, what are we celebrating?" Hope asked.

Just then two very handsome men entered the room.

"Ahhh. You must be Mrs. Darroff," said the taller of the two men.

The other chimed in, "You're much more beautiful in per- son. Pictures don't do you justice." He reached for her hand and kissed it.

"Okay, fellas, This is *my* wife, Hope. Hope, this is Brad Anderson and Fred Neilson."

The taller man was Brad, and Fred was average height. Both were impeccably dressed in tailor-made suits and shirts with cufflinks. Both wore two-toned shoes, and neither wore a wed- ding ring.

"Well, we're glad you could make it to the celebration," Fred said excitedly. "We are so excited about the three new projects

we just won, we wanted to have a little celebration and thank the staff for all their help."

"Well, I'm glad I came too," Hope replied sarcastically as she looked over at John. He just gave her a smirk and said nothing.

By the end of the luncheon, Hope learned that this new com- pany had expanded and the three new projects were all outside of Pennsylvania. They won a project for airport expansion in Atlanta, a major bridge construction project in New York, and had a gov- ernment contract in Maryland with NASA. She couldn't get too much information of that one. She found out that Brad was from Atlanta and Fred was from New York. The three of them joined forces about a year ago to make bids on those projects. Combining their resources made them better candidates to meet the minor- ity participation goals of these projects. They didn't need to be women owned, just minority. That's why he cut her out of the company. She couldn't believe it. If she hadn't walked in to sur- prise her husband and take him to lunch, she would have never known what was going on. She also learned that John planned to stay in Atlanta throughout the duration of the project, which was scheduled to take three years! He never mentioned a word to her about any of this! She was furious, but maintained her composure throughout the afternoon.

I'm gonna give it to him when he gets home tonight, she thought to herself. When she got home, Hazel told her that John called and said he had to go out of town tonight for business in Atlanta.

"He said he would call you later this evening, Mrs. Darroff." Hope went to her room wondering why he hadn't called her cell phone. She was about to undress when her cell phone rang.

"Hey, Hope! How do you like your new look?" It was Brenda. "Oh, hi, Brenda. I like it just fine."

"Well, you don't sound excited. Listen, let's meet for cocktails at Maggiano's so I can check you out. Meet me there in an hour." And she hung up, meaning she wasn't taking no for an answer. Hope touched up her hair and make-up and headed out the door.

"I love it!" exclaimed Brenda. "Still a little reserved, but there's a big difference. I love the hair! The highlights help bring out your skin tone, and the blunt cut outlines your pretty little face! You look fabulous! But I'm sensing…something's not right. What's going on with you?"

The waitress came over, and Brenda ordered two cosmopolitans. "I went to the office to surprise John today. Only I was the one who got the shock of my life." She explained the entire scenario to Brenda, who was now ordering a second round of cosmos.

"Honey. You *always* got to have a backup plan. Plan B, C, D, and E. Don't put all your eggs in one basket. Men have a history of leaving their wives destitute while they run off with all the money and a new young wife."

"I don't think John would—" Hope started to say but Brenda cut her off.

"I'm not saying John would do that, but you never know. Tell me, do you have a separate account of your own?"

Hope shook her head no.

"Have you considered starting your own business or doing anything else without your husband?"

Hope shook her head again.

"Listen, once Adam started making his millions, I made him finance my business and get me clients. Now I make my own millions outside of him. I have a major client in Dubai. I'll be leaving for Dubai in a few weeks and will be there indefinitely." She knew Hope had no clue about the double life both their husbands led. Brenda couldn't bring herself to tell her. She didn't think Hope would be able to handle it. That news would surely crush her to pieces. The woman would probably have a nervous breakdown. She suspected that John was a snake as well as a liar and had plans to take the money and leave Hope clueless. He had no conscience. Always talking about his church and being a deacon. She knew he was mean and nasty from the first time she met him. She felt sorry for Hope, who really tried to be the good little wife and mother and believed her husband loved her and would never do some underhanded stuff like she just described. Even though Hope had seen it for herself, she was still in denial. Brenda didn't know how to get through to her.

"Listen, Hope, you've spent the past fifteen years living your life according to John's wishes. What did you want to do with your life before you met him?

Hope thought for a second then said, "I wanted to be a lawyer." "Well, it's time you started working on that."

Brenda was right. It was time for Hope to start making her own dreams come true. She only had an associate's degree, so she would have to go back to school and get her bachelor's, then take the LSATS, and three more years of law school. She could do it!

"Okay! I'll do it!" she screamed.

Brenda made a final toast. "To you, girl! To your future. May

God bless you."

Hope was surprised because she knew that Brenda wasn't really "into God" as she put it. "Thanks, Brenda. That's means a lot."

Brenda hugged Hope really hard before they departed. She knew this was probably the last time they'd see each other. She had grown to really like her, but she would not be the one to tell her the truth about the life she was living in. Shit, Adam was just about totally out of the closet now. Although he was no longer involved with Doug, he was hanging out with an openly gay crowd of black men now. Brenda thought the breakup with Doug nearly killed Adam. He had grown despondent and lost interest in everything, including his business. The board of directors decided to vote him out as president, but he still receives a salary and generous bonuses, but he is not the same. Brenda could no longer live the life. Their daughters were all grown-up and aware of their father's lifestyle. One lives in Norway with her husband, and the other was traveling through Europe. There was no reason for Brenda to stick around. She was actually leaving for Dubai in the morning and had no intention to ever return to these United States of America, but she didn't want to tell Hope. She feared that conversation would lead her to telling the entire story, and she wasn't ready to do that.

John checked into a suite at the Sheraton Hotel downtown. He wasn't scheduled to be in Atlanta until next Thursday, but he didn't feel like facing Hope and her questions. He'd think of a good story and call her later. Tonight he would relax in his suite and check out the newest hot spots in center city. It had been a while since he had perused the streets of Philadelphia. He had been busy being initiated into the new world that he was now a part of. He missed the thrill of the streets;

prowling and just the animal-like hunt and the fierce spur-of-the-moment type of sex that the street encounters provided. Oh, he enjoyed the new life and its perks, but the old days had their perks too. He may have never met Brad Anderson if Adam hadn't brought him in. He and Brad hit it right off. They didn't have a sexual encounter, because they were both top men. However, once they started talking about their plan to form a company together and expand outside of Philadelphia, the idea just took off.

It was Brad who brought Fred into the picture because of his expertise in engineering and his success in the real estate indus- try. John wasn't sure if Fred was in the life or not, but he didn't really care. All he wanted was a good partner to help him expand his company and lifestyle. John hadn't had sex with Hope or any other woman in over a year. After Hope signed that big contract, he tried keeping her satisfied by watching his porn late at night in the den, then went to bed thinking of one of the men in the movies. He would take Hope from the back, penetrating her as if she were a man. But soon, he became so engrossed in business, starting the new company, and working on bids for those three contracts that he had no time or interest in any sex at all. Tonight, he would relax, order room service, and have a nice hot bath. He never called Hope as he had promised.

Hope played a few games of UNO with the girls before they went up to their rooms. She really enjoyed being able to spend quality time with them. They still needed her guidance, maybe even more since they were now teenagers. Soon they would be out and off to college. It was around 10:00 p.m., and John still hadn't called. She decided to take a bath and try to relax. She was still taken aback from what she learned today. Even though John made it seem as if everything was basically the same, she had an uneasy feeling. As soon as she got out of the tub, her cell phone rang. She answered, and an unfamiliar voice said, "Hello, may I speak with Hope please?"

"This is Hope. Who is this please?"

"Oh, hi, this is Ray, from the Bahamas. Remember me?"

Hope laughed, "Of course I remember you, Ray. It's nice to hear from you. How are you?"

She was really happy to hear from him after not hearing from John. Just the sound of his voice was soothing medicine to her heart. They talked for over two hours. Hope had not laughed so much in years. When they hung up, it was past midnight, and Hope realized that John still hadn't called. Somehow, his call didn't seem so important anymore. She turned off the lights and fell into a blissful sleep.

The next day after getting the girls off to school, she called
Patty and told her about what she learned.

"Girl. I don't trust that nigga as far as I can throw his ass! You better get that shit checked out. Sounds like he's setting him- self up to have 100 percent of the business and leave you with *zero*. Nothing! Do you hear me, Hope! Don't be stupid! He will take everything and leave you with nothing—or at least try to. Remember Bernadine from *Waiting to Exhale*. Well, this ain't no damn movie. This is your life. I gotta go to a meeting but will call you tomorrow. I'm eager to hear what you plan to do. Love you! Smooches!" And she hung up.

Hope knew Patty was right. She picked up the phone to call Brenda, but got her answering machine. "Hello, you've reached Brenda Strong. I am relocating to Dubai and cannot be reached at the moment. Please leave a message and your phone number, and I will get back to you as soon as I settle in. Thanks!" *Beep*.

"Hey, Brenda! This is Hope. I didn't realize you were leaving so soon. Please call me as soon as you can."

She thought about calling John but then decided against it. Instead, she decided to go into town and shop. She decided to go into the bank first to get some cash. As she crossed Broad Street she spotted Adam Long waving to her from across the street. He ran up to her looking handsome as ever in his finely tailored suit.

"Hey, girl!" he exclaimed, sounding overly feminine. "And how are those beautiful girls of yours?"

Was it her imagination, or was Adam sounding gay? He looked the same, but his mannerisms and speech told an entirely different story.

"They're fine," Hope replied as she began walking to the bank. Adam walked alongside her and continued talking. "Girl, you
look fabulous! I haven't seen you in a while. I'm glad to see you're
looking well considering the situation with your company."

"What situation? Everything is going quite well, Adam. As a matter of fact, John started a new company and has three major contracts that expand from New York to Atlanta."

"Honey, I'm not talking about the new company. I'm talking about your company. The contracts that your company had with mine have gone sour. The company was unable to complete the job, and we had to sue and replace you with another contractor. Your company is bankrupt, honey. You didn't know?"

Adam knew completely well that Hope didn't have a clue about the situation with the company any more than she knew about the double life her husband led. He felt bad for her and felt at least he should tell her about the company. As for the dou- ble life, well, he purposely acted extra flaming when he saw her. Maybe she'd put two and two together. But by the look on her face, she might not; she was obviously in shock about the news he'd just shared.

"N…n…no," Hope stammered. "I didn't know." She was at the teller now. She rarely went to the bank or carried cash. She used credit cards for everything, but today she wanted cash. She filled out a withdrawal slip for $1,000, and the teller told her that the account had been closed. Hope stood there shocked.

"Come on, honey. Let me take you to lunch," Adam said as he led her out the door.

"No, I can't eat. I need to go home," Hope replied.

John pulled out his money clip and gave her $500. "Here, honey, take this. I'm sorry you found out this way, but you must be the only person in the city who didn't know what was happen- ing with your own company. You take care of yourself." Then he walked south on Broad Street, leaving Hope standing there in a complete state of shock.

She must have stood there for ten minutes before she could even think. She got her car and drove to the office where Sharon greeted her in the lobby.

"Hi, Hope! How are you? You look great!"

"Thanks, Sharon. Can you come with me to my office, please?" Hope closed the door behind them and asked Sharon if she had any paperwork on the convention center and stadium contracts.

"Well, I have the contracts and copies of the lawsuit. All of the financial records have been subpoenaed and are with the accountant and the auditor. We're still waiting for a court date."

Tears began streaming down Hope's face as she sunk down into the chair. "You didn't know?" Sharon said slowly. "I thought you knew. That's why John said you two were starting a new com- pany. He told us that you said that this had been a learning expe- rience and agreed to let this company die so we could start the new company and get those contracts started. I'm so sorry, Hope. I thought you knew."

Sharon was sincerely sorry for Hope. She realized what a bas- tard John was, when he ended their affair and acted as if it never happened. He treated her indifferently, but she kept her posi- tion as office manager and did her job well. She knew about all the dirt he did and how slimy he was with the handling of the money from those two contracts. She knew exactly why they ran out of money because of his mismanagement of funds, but as an employee she could not testify against the company. Now she understood what he was planning to do to Hope. She owned 51 percent of the company so she would take all the blame for the loss contracts. Sharon got up and left. All she could say was that she was sorry as she left Hope in her office sobbing.

Hope went home, got into bed, and stayed there in the fetal position for two days. She couldn't pray. She couldn't eat. She couldn't talk and could barely think. She thought she was los- ing her mind. Her children tried to take care of her, bringing her food, tea, water, and juice trying to keep her hydrated. They wanted to call G'mom, but Hope forbade them. They finally called her cousin Patty, who arrived about thirty minutes later. When she looked at Hope, she already knew what happened, so she didn't say anything; she just held Hope, rocked her, gave her liquids, and told jokes for about two hours.

Finally Hope laughed at the joke about the wife who asked her husband what he would do if she hit the lottery. He said, "I'd take half and leave."

She said, "*Good*! I just won $10! Here's $5. Now get the fuck out!"

Hope laughed so hard she had to pee. While she was washing her hands she looked at her reflection in the mirror. "Who am I, and what the hell am I doing here? How did I allow myself to get into this predicament?" She washed her make-up–smeared face and brushed her teeth. Then she decided to take a shower for the first time in two days. Meanwhile, Patty made her bed, cleared all the clutter from her room, and put a pot of green chamomile tea, toast, and orange juice on a tray.

"Be right out," Hope called from the bathroom. She looked in the mirror at herself and said, "God, I know you didn't bring me this far to leave me. I trust you."

Hope emerged from the bathroom looking much better but still stressed. "Well, you look much better. Here have some tea and toast. You gotta eat something." The two women ate and

drank in silence, each deep in their own thoughts. Patty was thinking about the baby growing inside her and the proposal of marriage that she received from the baby's father last night. She didn't know if she was ready for family life, and now looking at her cousin, she was absolutely sure that she would have to have a prenup drawn up for him to sign. Her assets were significantly more than his, and she needed to protect herself. She really liked him though and was kind of excited about starting a new chapter in her life. Excited, but afraid at the same time. She wanted to share this news with her closest friend and cousin, but now didn't seem to be the right time.

Hope was thinking about her lying, low-down husband. He thought he could get away with this? She was going to file for divorce immediately and take at least half of the money he had with his new company. He would not leave her high and dry. She finally spoke. "I'm going to file for a divorce."

"I think that's a great idea. I know a great family law attorney. We can call her right now if you'd like."

Later that afternoon, Hope found herself sitting in the office of Maryann Skikowski, a divorce attorney, explaining her situation to Lauren Steinberg.

"Well, first, I want you to know that your situation is not unique, Hope. May I call you Hope? Many women find them- selves in this type of mess after they've helped their husbands through school or become successful, and then the husband wants to take all the money and leave her poor and destitute. The good thing for you is that your company was a corporation, and as a corporation no individual is financially responsible. The courts will take any and everything that is in the corporation's name, but your personal assets are protected as long as you didn't sign any

personal guarantees, offer any personal property as collateral, sign any contracts in your own name, or use personal credit cards or loans to fund your business."

"We used the house as collateral when we first started the business, but I'm pretty sure that loan was paid off," Hope replied.

"Well, let's hope so. As far as the other business goes, if your husband owns any percentage, then you are entitled to a portion of the total assets of the company and anything else that is in his name."

Hope and Patty were relieved to hear that news. They went to lunch and shopped. She had almost forgotten all about Adam Strong's persona until she started to relay the entire series of events to Patty. They both fell out laughing at the idea of Adam being gay.

"But he's so fine." Hope laughed.

"Those are the ones!" Patty replied. "I guess Brenda found out, and that's why she moved to Dubai."

"What? She moved to Dubai? Wow. At least she got paid out the deal. We gonna make sure you get paid too. You deserve to live comfortably. Listen, why don't we take a getaway to the Bahamas? You could use a little R&R before this war you're about to fight."

Hope agreed.

They continued shopping, but all of a sudden Hope wasn't excited about shopping anymore. She was looking forward to getting away but not excited about shopping for some reason. All she wanted was a new sweat suit to wear on the plane.

"What's wrong, Hope? If it's money you're worried about, don't. You charge anything you want on my credit card. This trip is my treat, a sort of celebration of your new life."

"No. It's not the money, Patty. I'm not sure what it is. It's just like I really need this trip but"—she had to sit down. She felt weak in the knees. Something was terribly wrong, but she couldn't put her finger on it.

"Okay. You definitely need this trip. I'll book the flight and make reservations tonight, and Friday we will be out! We'll be two Bahamas mamas for three days and two nights!"

Hope just paid for her sweat suit and rode home in silence. She started packing as soon as she got home. She was looking forward to the trip. All this was beginning to weigh in on her. She still hadn't heard from John, but she would not be the one to call. He knew exactly what he had done. She had to now face the fact that this man couldn't have possibly ever loved her. She wasted sixteen years of her life trying to be perfect for him, and he never cared. Now he wanted to just leave her and the kids high and dry. She knew he had no intention of ever coming back home. She had a good mind to burn all his stuff. She smiled as she imagined herself doing what Bernadine did in the movie *Waiting to Exhale*. Then she would sit on the couch and watch *Nanny and the Professor*. Then she just started laughing hysteri- cally. The girls came into her room to see what was so funny. Hope just kept laughing, and soon all three of them were rolling on the bed cracking up. It felt good.

"Call G'mom and see if you can stay the weekend with her. I'm going out of town with Aunt Patty. After that, order a pizza and hot wings, and let's have movie night."

"Okay, Mommy."

Hope loved her girls more than life itself. They had not even asked about their father, and he'd been gone for almost a week. They were old enough to know that something was going on between Mommy and Daddy, but they never asked questions. Most of their time was spent at G'mom's these days. They were

good girls, never gave Hope one minute of grief. She would make sure to spend more quality time with them from now on. Right now she was going to finish packing. Then she decided to call her mom herself.

"Hey, Mom. Can the girls stay with you this weekend? Patty and I are going on a little getaway."

"Yeah, Hope. I told them yes already. I haven't seen much of you lately. I need you to come over and help me with some papers. I need to make a living will and am thinking of getting one of those reverse mortgages. Can you come over next week and help me review this stuff?"

"Sure, Mom, but why would you want to get a reverse mort- gage? I think it would be better for you to move to a retire- ment complex."

"Oh, I never thought about that. We can discuss it next week. Where are you girls going? And where's John? The girls said he hasn't been home in days. They also said you've not been eating and crying a lot. You never call me to talk anymore, Hope. I just keep you in prayer. I understand sometimes you just don't want to talk, but you know you can always come to your momma, right?"

"Yes, Mom. I'm sorry. I promise I'll come over next Tuesday, and we'll spend the entire day together—just you and me talking. I love you, Mommy."

"Love you too, baby."

John woke up feeling refreshed. He hadn't felt this good in a long time. Living at home with a wife whom he now hated with a passion and having to wake up with her every morning pretending that their life together was perfect was beginning to wear on him. He was very close to living his life free from the burden of the

last year. He spent the day pampering himself. First, a massage, manicure, pedicure, and then he went to the sauna. He took a nap, had dinner, got dressed, and perused the nightlife up and down Locust Street.

There were lots of young boys out and plenty of trannies. John wasn't into either of these types. He liked men who looked and acted like men but loved to be on the bottom. He passed all the newer spots where the patrons poured to the outside streets attracting drivers who pulled up proposition them. He saw many cars lined up with drivers being serviced by young boys. Mostly the young ones were into this scene. He ended up at an old famil- iar spot down Fourteenth and Ludlow and walked in. Here the men were all well dressed. Some were feminine, and others very masculine, but all looked "normal."

John sat down at the bar, ordered his usual Courvoisier on the rocks, and looked around. He started drinking over the last few years. He saw Brad at the far end of the bar talking to a hand- some light-skinned man with hazel eyes. He smiled to himself. This was where he actually met Brad. They weren't attracted to each other, but they struck up a conversation and learned that they had a lot in common. Both men were married to women who had no idea of their secret lifestyle. Both had businesses in the construction industry, and both were trying to expand but needed to partner with another company to increase chances of acquiring capital for larger projects. Brad's wife was not involved in his business though. He told John it was bad business to have your wife involved and helped him form the new company. He advised John not to be an officer of the company but to be an employee, until he divorced Hope. Then she wouldn't be entitled to any of the assets of the company. She could only maybe get ali- mony based on his $400,000 salary. After they divorced, then John would become an officer of the company and receive his share of the company's assets, which by then would be very substantial.

Brad excused himself from his conquest for the night when he spotted John.

"Hey, partner," he said as they shook hands. "Getting in a lit- tle recreation before heading down to Atlanta, huh? You're gonna love Atlanta, man. Places like this are a dime a dozen. And the women down there don't mind being beards. Most bitches only in relationships for the money anyway, so they're down as long as they are well compensated. My wife? She allows Brad to be Brad, and she does her thing—whatever it is—and we're cool. She makes her appearances for dinners, fund-raisers, and business functions—keeping my image in, and that's that. Some bitches even join in with their husbands and love threesomes and all- around orgies. But your wife? Man, she doesn't have a clue, does she? I think she actually really loves you, John."

John had to agree. Hope really did love him. He loved her too once. He thought she could take away his sexual appetite for men because the first time they made love, he came twice. He had never came twice before. Sex with her was amazing before the babies were born. She gained weight, but he was still very much attracted to her; however, her sexual appetite diminished, and she would never ever have anal sex. One night after she refused anal sex, he went downtown and picked up a guy off the street, and they had sex.

After two years of not having sex with men, this encounter was the most exciting and satisfying sexual experience of his life. He was back in the life from that point on. Yes, he once loved Hope, but now he'd grown to hate her. He despised her but loved his girls. He would always take care of them. Hope was just too damn naive. She really thought their image of a perfect family was real. She lived in a fantasy world. She was wrapped up in the church and her little make-believe world. She needed to take a lesson from Tina and learn that love has absolutely *nothing* to do with it. She would never fit into his real world. He wouldn't leave her high and dry though. He would agree to pay her alimony until she remarried. Maybe she would actually find somebody who lived in the same fantasy world she lived in. As for John, he was living in the real world—a world where participating in debauchery was the initiation to money and power. That's the life he wanted, and now he was well on his way. He could never be content with just a home, a savings account, and a beautiful, lov- ing, and faithful wife.

All his life he had to hide his appetite for men. Well, now he had found a world where he not only didn't have to hide it, but this appetite was also what was helping him to get ahead in life. He was moving forward and had no time to look back. He decided then and there that he would not call Hope and come up with an explanation. She'd find out soon enough what was going down. He'd go to Atlanta where the company had already purchased a penthouse, and that would be his new home. He'd call the girls in a month or so, after school got out for the summer and have them come down for a few weeks. He'd explain things to them before serving Hope with the divorce papers.

He raised his glass to Brad and said, "Here's to new beginnings."

As soon as they arrived and checked in, all Hope wanted to do was sleep. And sleep she did. She slept from 6:00 p.m. Friday until 2:00 p.m. Saturday. She woke up to an empty, freezing-cold room. Patty left a note saying she'd be poolside; she also left the air-conditioner on high. Hope turned off the air and jumped in a warm shower; letting the water run through her hair and down her body was therapeutic. She stood in the shower until the water began to run cold. She got dressed and went out on the balcony where there was a perfect view of the ocean. She just stood there watching the beauty of God's hands, wondering if He had gotten an artist's block when it came to her life. In her eyes, her life was life a watercolor painting that had gotten wet, and all the beautiful colors were now dripping down the paper, running into each other making a chaotic mess. That's how her life felt—like a chaotic mess.

Well, one thing was for sure, and two things were for certain: God didn't give us more than we can handle, and she didn't think things could get much worse. Still she had this nagging feeling in her gut, like something was terribly wrong. She decided to go down and get something to eat, but she didn't see Patty anywhere, so she took her food back up to the room, sat on the balcony, and ate. She bought a book and decided to sit there and read it: *A Day Late and a Dollar Short.* She couldn't remember the last time she actually read a good book.

Patty came back around 7:00 p.m. She spent the day snorke- ling and parasailing. She was such an adventurer. She told Hope to get dressed because she'd made reservations for them to eat at LaScalla's on the beach. She had a surprise.

Hope wasn't really hungry and didn't feel much like going out, but she did. They dined on a seafood feast of lobster, crab cakes, mussels, shrimps, and oysters. Patty ate like a horse as Hope nib- bled here and there.

"Okay, are you ready for my big surprise!" "Yes. What is it?"

"I'm pregnant! I'm four months pregnant!"

Hope's face finally lit up. "Oh, cousin! That's wonderful! A new baby. Do you know if it's a boy or a girl?"

"No, I want to be surprised. The father's name is Bob. He's an engineer for Merck. He asked me to marry him, but I don't know about all that. Just because I'm having his baby doesn't necessar- ily mean we have to get married. He's a pretty nice guy, but…I mean…a new baby *and* a new husband all at once? That's a bit much, don't you think?"

Hope just smiled. She was so happy for her cousin. Personally she didn't think

Patty was cut out to be a wife, not in the tradi- tional sense. She'd probably make a great mom though.

"I think you should follow your instincts. You're usually on point."

They continued talking over desert and coffee. Hope was enjoying herself but still felt uneasy in her spirit. She couldn't shake this feeling, and it stuck with her throughout the remain- der of their getaway all the way home. She hadn't been much fun on this trip, but Patty didn't seem to notice; she maintained her active lifestyle—pregnant and all.

Back at home, Hope was feeling rather normal as she unpacked. She did some laundry and took out lamb chops from the refrigerator to prepare for dinner. She planned to prepare the girls' favorite dinner: lamb chops, asparagus, and mashed pota- toes. She would pick the girls up, and they would go to the bakery and pick up desert. She checked the answering machine to see if there was any call from John. It had been over two weeks since her encounter with Adam and her visit to the office. There was no message from John, but there was a message from her attorney.

"Hello, Hope, this is Miriam Skikowski. I've done some research, and it seems that your house was put up as collateral for a loan that is in default. The loan was in the company's name, but since you put up a personal asset as collateral, you are in danger of losing it. Please give me a call at your earliest convenience so we can review your options."

What the hell? Hope thought. That's why she had that nagging feeling for the past few days. She was going to lose her home. She vaguely remembered that loan; it had been six or seven years ago, and John told her that it was paid in full. She never saw any bills from the loan company. All of his lies and deceptions were now coming to light.

"Well, the Word says that everything in the darkness will come to light," she said to herself. "I'm not even gonna worry about that; God can and will provide me with a new house, so I'm just gonna praise him through this circumstance because the devil is a liar!"

Just then the phone rang. "Hello?"

"Mom. Come to the hospital quick. Something is wrong with G'mom."

"What? What are you saying? What hospital? What's the matter?" Hope stammered. "What hospital?"

"Adelphia. Mommy, hurry! Something is wrong!" Kennedy hung up.

Hope turned off the broiler, grabbed her purse and keys, jumped in the car, and drove to the city. Once in the city it seemed like she caught every red light. Kennedy kept calling ask- ing where she was.

"I'm on my way." Why did they take her to Adelphia? They know how she hates that hospital. Boy, Hope knew she was gonna hear it when she got there. She'd make arrangement to have her transferred immediately.

Finally she pulled into the hospital's parking lot. "Lord, please let my mom be okay. Thank you."

She went straight to the emergency entrance. "I'm here for Bernie Hightower," she said.

Then a doctor came out and asked, "Are you her daughter?"

Hope nodded. "Yes."

"Well, we have a situation here. We think she has a blood clot and need your permission to give her a medication that may thin

the clot, or it may make it burst. There's a 50-50 chance if we administer this medication. Do we have your permission?"

"Yes, yes, of course," Hope replied.

"Okay, the other problem is that we can't find a heartbeat."

"What? What do you mean you can't find a heartbeat! Get in there and find it then!" Hope screamed. Her mind was not accepting what she had just been told. "Where are my daughters?"

"They're in the waiting room. Do you have any other family members, a husband, brothers, or sister that you want to call?"

"No. No one but us. Please administer the medication and let me know what happens." Then she went to the waiting room to find Kamari and Kennedy crying uncontrollably. A nurse was there with them offering them tea and water. She was trying to calm them down so they could tell her what happened when the doctor came in.

"I'm sorry, miss. We just pronounced your mother dead."

Season of Oppression

John loved Atlanta! He had finally found a place where he could truly be himself. He felt a sense of peace that he'd never felt before. Business was going well, and Brad had introduced him to some of the hot spots. He was enjoying himself and had quite a few flings before he met Ted. Ted was a cop who was married but was completely gay. His wife, Anna, had no idea that she was just a beard, even though they never had sex. She hit the lottery a few years ago and bought them a beautiful home in Decatur. She was the director of a Women's Resource Center that she founded after her divorce from an abusive husband. The center had programs to help women obtain skills and start their own business. She was always very busy with work and very active in her church. They had separate rooms because she liked having her own space. Ted worked the graveyard shift and spent most of his free time at John's condo. This man had John completely turned out; he was now a bottom and top with Ted. He never thought he'd enjoy having a dick up his ass, but one night in the heat of passion, Ted flipped him over and took his virginity. That night they slept entwined in each other's arms, and John was hooked.

They spent most of their free time together: shopping, dining out, going to the movies or theater. They weren't ashamed to be seen together, but never had PDAs (public display of affection). Until he met Ted, John had no interest in developing a relation- ship. He was fine enjoying a bunch of flings. He never spent the night with any of his lovers, but Ted had changed all of that. All that would have to end for the summer because his daughters were coming to stay with him. He hadn't seen them since Hope's mother's funeral. He stayed at the house with them and Hope for two weeks, cooking, cleaning, and packing up his belongings.

Hope was in a pretty bad shape, and the doctor had prescribed some heavy drugs that kept her in bed most of the time. The girls would take her meals to her, but she barely ate. One night she came into John's room with a knife, threatening to kill him for lying to her and allowing their home to be in jeopardy. He was able to talk her out it by apologizing and making her think that he wasn't aware that would happen. He assured her that he would never put her or the kids' welfare in jeopardy. She finally calmed down and went to bed. That night he left and never returned.

The next week he filed for divorce based on irreconcilable dif- ferences and offered to pay $5,000 per month in alimony and

$2,500 in child support. His lawyer was still waiting to hear back from Hope's lawyer, but in the meantime, she did agree to allow the girls to spend the summer in Atlanta with him. He still kept his secret life on the down low and started dating a woman named Terry. Terry was an aspiring actress and was only out to get whatever she could. She knew John was gay, but he had con- nections, looked good, and treated her well. John liked having a pretty young thing to take to parties, but Ted, on the other hand, was very jealous, Therefore, Terry never went to the house. John would have her meet the girls, though. He was sure they would get along well. Terry would be responsible for showing them a good time, keep them occupied, and John would compensate her

well for her role. Ted was upset about the summer arrangement, but he understood. He decided that he would tell his wife the truth about his lifestyle this summer. It was time.

As John drove to the airport to pick up the girls, he thought about how Brad was dragging his feet on the business side of things. He kept saying John should wait until the divorce was final before he came on as an officer in the company. John felt that if Hope's lawyer agreed to the alimony and child support, then it wouldn't make any difference. John was beginning to get skeptical about the whole business deal, but he still received his
$400,000 salary and lived in the penthouse rent free, so he had no complaints. Life was good. He had everything he'd ever wanted. Ted had filled the void of love and family. Being an only child he'd never really felt close to anyone. He left his mother's house when he was eighteen and had been on his own ever since and had never really opened up to anyone—not even Hope. In Ted, he had found a love that he never knew existed and he never wanted to lose it. One day he would tell his children the truth, but not this summer. This summer he would bond with them and allow them to get to know their father. He loved his girls and wanted to show them how a man should treat a woman. He would use Terry to show them.

"Daddy!" Kennedy screamed when she was him. She ran and hugged him so tight he lost his breath. She had always been a daddy's girl, even though she was the eldest.

Kamari was very nonchalant and aloof. "Hi, Daddy." Was all she said. He grabbed her and hugged her, but she didn't hug back.

"Well, let's get your luggage so we can get out of this airport." "Yes, I want to get out of here and see MLK Park, and can we
go eat at Gladys Knight and Ron Winans Chicken & Waffles
place, Dad? I'm starving!" Kennedy was so excited.

"Sure, baby. Anything you want. Kamari, do you want to do anything special?"

"No. not really."

That was all she said. John was heartbroken. Kennedy had gotten the best of his fathering years. Kamari missed a lot. He vowed to make it up to her this summer.

They spent the afternoon downtown eating and shopping. Kamari started loosening up while they were shopping. He took them to the outlets where she bought all the Aeropostale her heart desired. Kamari was more into sportswear, and Kennedy was more like her mother, conservative and ladylike. Every outfit she picked out required accessories. She spent about three hours shopping in different stores, while Kamari was content with all her items being purchased from one store. That gave them a little time to spend together alone. At first it was a little awkward. John couldn't come up with any topic that seemed to interest her. He watched her as she listened to him politely, but her mind or heart wasn't in it. She was busy watching the boys walked by, playing a game of cat and mouse with her eyes and body language to seek if she could get their attention.

Finally! John thought. *He'd talk about boys!* His heart began beating rapidly. Would he handle that conversation knowing his own story? Atlanta was known as the gay capital for black men and boys. He couldn't stand to think of his daughter falling for a guy like him. It made him sad to think of that scenario. How could he educate his daughters about this life and how to recog- nize the behavior? The very thought of it terrified him because he knew that sometime in the very near future he would have to tell his daughters the complete truth about his lifestyle.

Hope drove through the cemetery to her mother's grave, still unable to grasp the fact that she was gone. It had been a whole year since she and her daughters sat in the hospital waiting room stunned by the sudden and untimely death of their matriarch. The entire year was still a blur to her. So much had happened. She had to keep herself together to plan the funeral and in trying to keep the girls together. John never even called but showed up the day of the funeral to play the part of a devoted son-in-law and doting father. She allowed him to sit in the pew with both the girls between them. He held and comforted them, while Hope sat stoic throughout the entire ceremony as if she was in a dream. It felt like a nightmare. She didn't cry. She acted like an event planner as she planned the service and repast with precision and meticulous attention to every detail. She didn't break down and actually didn't even cry until three weeks later. Patty suggested that she seek counseling. Hope took offense, and that discussion erupted into a huge fight, and they hadn't spoken since. Hope did send a gift to her baby. She heard that Patty had eloped a few months ago. She kept saying she was gonna call her but hadn't done so yet. She missed her cousin, but she had so much on her plate right now and didn't want all those people in her ear. She had to handle things her way and on her terms.

Hope pulled up to the familiar grave site that she'd visited far too often over the last twelve months. She pulled her chair out of the car and sat down with her cup of coffee, which was laced with brandy. This was her new morning drink.

"Well, Mommy, I can't believe it's been almost a whole year since you've been gone. I miss you so much. So much has hap- pened since you've been gone. We lost the house because John put it up for collateral to fund one of the company's projects and never made good on the loan. Then the snake let the company go into bankruptcy with me as majority owner. Then he started a new company with multimillion-dollar contracts in three dif-

ferent states. Mommy, he drives a Maserati, and I'm still driv- ing my same ole BMW I40. You were right about him from the beginning, but I wouldn't listen. You didn't harp on it though, just loved and supported me through my terrible decision. He filed for divorce. Can you believe *he* wants to divorce *me*! It should be the other way around. Crazy as it may sound I *still* don't want a divorce. I guess because I don't know any other life. I've been his wife for over sixteen years, and I don't know anything else. I won't contest it though. He can have a divorce. He's been living in Atlanta with his new girlfriend, so I have grounds for spousal support. The girls went down there for the summer, so I'll have time to get myself together. Maybe I'll go back to school, become a lawyer like I've always talked about."

She sipped the last of her drink as tears streamed down her cheeks. "I still don't understand why God is allowing all this stuff to happen to me—all at the same time. I just don't understand, Mommy. I've always tried to be good, do the right things. I was a faithful wife, devoted mother, and Christian. It seems like the race is actually given to the swift. I can't even pray anymore." She got up, folded her chair, got in her car, lit up a joint, and drove home.

For the past seven months, she started her day at 5:00 a.m. with the brandy-and-coffee drink and a joint. It was the only thing she looked forward to. After she sent the kids off the school, she'd smoke another joint and just lay in the bed all day. This had been her routine. She didn't answer the phone. She didn't shower or even brush her teeth half the time. She barely ate, and the sweatpants that she wore every day were now falling off her behind. Now, with the girls away she didn't even have to go out for anything.

Today was the first day she'd come out in a few days, and she went straight to the cemetery. Somehow, she always felt a little better after sitting there talking. When she got home she took a

good look at her house. It looked like a cyclone had gone through it. When she and the girls moved into her mom's house, it was a major transition. All of their belongings plus her mom's stuff were just piled up everywhere. Hope decided to make some cof- fee and get started cleaning up. She discovered that she was out of coffee, cream, and sugar. She had nothing in the refrigerator except a jar of pickles and two cans of Pepsi. She decided to go to the supermarket.

On her way out she walked past a mirror. She stopped, reversed, and took a good look at herself. She looked a mess. She decided to take a shower and put some clean clothes on before going out. Hope didn't want people thinking that she was fall- ing apart—even if she was. She thought about calling her aunt. Her mother's only sister, Ann, who is Patty's mother, called her at least twice a week to check on her. Hope never answered the phone, so her answering machine was full of messages. She sus- pected Aunt Ann would pay her a visit soon because she couldn't leave any more messages. She made sure that her aunt Ann was on her calling list later that day. Hope sure didn't want a surprise visit with her house looking the way it did.

As she started toward the checkout line she heard someone calling her name.

"Hope Highsmith?"

She looked, and there was one of her best childhood friends Sheryl. They'd been friends all through elementary, middle, and high school. Yes, Sheryl was truly a blast from the past—a past that Hope left far behind when she married John.

"Girl, I haven't seen you in so long! I'm so sorry about your mom. I just moved back into Philly last week and heard about it." Sheryl had also heard about Hope's marriage and the busi- ness. Rumors were spreading that Hope was losing her mind. She didn't look too bad though. She was still very pretty. Hope had always been pretty. All the boys always liked her. That Hope always had the fly guys with the money and drugs. Their young adulthood days were wild and crazy. They even started working in a strip club together and made lots of money for a few years. The men *loved* Hope. She had a sweet voice and knew just the right things to say to make a man do whatever she wanted him to do. That's one of the reasons why Sheryl hung out with her—along with the fact that Sheryl had a crush on Hope. She didn't realize it at the time. She just thought that she liked Hope and enjoyed her company. But as Sheryl got older, she realized that she had an attraction toward women and that Hope had been her first crush.

When Hope met John, Sheryl hung out with them for a while, but then Hope began to change. John wasn't the typical type of man that Hope hung out with. He was a small-time drug dealer with a steady job as an electrician. He didn't really want to be in the game; he was just a wannabe.

Soon Hope got pregnant, stopped partying, and got married. That's when she and Sheryl lost contact. Hope was off the map. Nobody really heard much from her in years, but the crew kept up with her accomplishments. She had become a sort of celeb- rity. Sheryl always knew Hope would be somebody, so when she saw her and John picture in the *Adelphia Magazine* as one of Philadelphia's "power couples," she wasn't a bit surprised. Hope seemed happy to see Sheryl and to have someone to talk to. They continued to chat as they walked toward Hope's car when sud- denly Hope burst into tears. Sheryl grabbed her and hugged her.

"I just don't know what to do, Sheryl. I don't know what to do," she kept repeating over and over. Sheryl didn't want to leave her alone, so she told Hope she would follow her home so they could talk. She couldn't believe the mess that she walked into. Hope's house had always been immaculate. She sat and watched Hope light up a joint and put on a pot of coffee.

"Excuse the mess, Sheryl. I just can't seem to get motivated to do anything. This is a really hard time for me, and I have no one to help me."

"Well, first of all, smoking weed makes you lazy." Sheryl laughed as she pulled out a little plastic bag of white powder. "You need something to give you a burst of energy to start clean- ing up this mess." She pulled out a $20 bill and rolled it up. Then she pulled out a little compact mirror and razor, poured some of the powder onto the mirror, cut it up, and separated it into four thick lines. She snorted one up each nostril then passed the rolled-up bill over to Hope.

"Take a snort, honey. It'll make you feel better."

At this point Hope was willing to try anything to make her feel better, so she took the powder up each nostril and immedi- ately had a feeling of euphoria. It felt good. She sat and relished that feeling as Sheryl prepared more lines for them to snort. Before she knew it hours had passed. They had talked and remi- nisced about old times; the kitchen and dining room were clean, clothes sorted in piles to keep and piles to go to the Salvation Army. Yeah. She liked that cocaine high. She didn't feel depressed and was full of energy. Sheryl pulled out a joint and lit it up.

"Time to wind it down for the night," she said as she took a long, hard drag then passed it to Hope.

"You smoke a nice joint and have a glass of wine to wind down. Then sleep like a baby." She pulled out a $50 bag and put it on the table. "Keep this around; you may want some tomorrow to help you finish cleaning up in here."

"Where did you get it from?" Hope asked.

"Oh, my boyfriend Ray deals. He keeps me supplied, so don't worry about it. This is on my girlfriend. Call me if you want some more, but take it easy, and I'll see you tomorrow. This should last you a few days."

After Sheryl left, Hope lay down and fell into a deep sleep. When she woke the next morning, the first thing she thought about was the bag of coke Sheryl left on the dining room table. She sat up in bed and looked around at the mess surrounding her. Each night she had pushed the pile of clothes, books, and whatever else was on her bed to one side and slept on the other. Today she would tackle her room. She got up and went to get the cocaine so she could get started. After about four hours, she'd gotten all the clothes, books, papers, and junk sorted out and neatly put away with the help of Sheryl.

"Here, I'll leave this bag with you." Sheryl put a $20 bag of cocaine on the dining room table. "I have to go handle some busi- ness. I'll give you a call later."

When Sheryl left, Hope took another snort. By the time the bag was empty, she'd bagged all the clothes to take to the Salvation Army, wiped down all the furniture, and cleaned the windows and blinds. The other bag of cocaine was almost fin- ished. She put it up, smoked a joint, and made herself a sand- wich. She was feeling really good about getting the place cleaned up. She figured she was on a roll, so she took two more noseful and started cleaning again. By the time the bag was empty, shed cleaned the entire upstairs, including wiping down the walls and woodworks. She looked at the clock and it was nine thirty. Happy and content with what she'd accomplished that day, she sat down and lit another joint. Then the phone rang.

"Hey, girl! What you doing?

"Hey, Sheryl, I'm just winding down. I cleaned the entire upstairs and bagged up six bags for the Salvation Army. Just smoking a J now and getting ready to take a bath. What's up?"

"It's first Friday, girl. My man gives parties at his club every first Friday. You should come hang out. When's the last time you been out?"

Hope honestly couldn't remember the last time she'd been out to a club. "It's been at least sixteen years, Sheryl. I don't even have anything to wear."

"Not a problem. What are you? A size 10? I have some size 10s in my closet. I'm a 4 now, but I couldn't part with my nice, expensive size 10 clothes. I'll be right over. We'll have a ball!"

After they hung up, Hope jumped in the shower and started working on her hair and make-up when the phone rang again. *That must be Sheryl; she should be here by now*, she thought.

"Hello? Oh. Hi, Aunt Ann. Yes, yes, I received all you mes- sages. I'm sorry I didn't call you back, but I was going to call you tonight. Yes, I know the machine is full. Yes, I'm fine. As a matter of fact, I'm getting ready to go out. You remember Sheryl, the girl I used to hang with in high school? Yes, the one whose mom ran the number house. Yes, well, I ran into her at the supermar- ket, and we're hanging out tonight. Yes, ma'am, I know I have to watch the company I keep. Yes, I know that I must move forward and not backward, but we're just going out to a party. Yes, I'll be careful. I promise I will call you in a few days. Love you too, Auntie. Bye."

Sheryl and Hope arrived at the club after midnight, and the line to get in was around the corner. Sheryl walked right up to the front and was escorted to the VIP section. She made sure Hope was right beside her. When they got into the VIP section, all eyes were on Hope. She was looking ravishing in a black catsuit with a crocodile belt and shoes. There were other women there, but Hope was new, fresh meat.

"Damn, Sheryl! Is that Hope?" one of the guys asked.

Hope recognized him. His name was Tyrone. He tried to get with Hope back in the day, but he wasn't her speed. He was a small-time weed dealer. Hope could see that he had graduated.

"Hey, Hope. You remember me? Tyrone from Seventy-Sixth Avenue? Yeah, I was small-time then. I've moved up, baby. This is my club. Girl, you look better than ever. Here, come over here and sit next to me, Miss Hope. What's your last name again?"

"Hope Darroff," a deep voice from the crowd answered. A tall figure emerged from the crowd and Hope recognized him imme- diately. It was Ray from the Bahamas. He took her hand and kissed it.

"Y'all know each other?" Sheryl asked.

"We met once. Had lunch together. How are you, Hope? You look good. It's nice to see you again."

"Hey, Ray, it's nice to see you too."

Ray kissed Sheryl on the forehead and whispered in her ear, "Hey, baby. There's some new stuff in the back room for you. Go check it out. I'm having packages put together for you to sell this week."

Sheryl immediately went to the back room. She forgot all about Hope and her familiarity with her man. All she had on her mind was the new batch of cocaine. She wanted a hit. Ray knew that she would be back there for the rest of the night. He wanted to talk to Hope. He hadn't seen her since the Bahamas. He called her a few times, but she never answered or returned his calls. For some reason he couldn't get her off his mind. He read about her company's problems in the newspapers. That was the last time he tried to call, but the phone had been cut off. He was both surprised and happy to see her show up in his club, but with Sheryl? How did they know each other? Sheryl was a coke fiend and a hoe. Just about every guy and girl in the VIP section had slept with her. She was a hell of a saleswoman though. She could push a whole kilo of coke in a week. He kept her close, and she made him lots of money. He couldn't take his eyes off Hope. She looked like a fresh fish out of water, but she looked good in that catsuit.

"So, Mrs. Darroff. We finally meet again. I see you've met my manager, Tyrone." He tactfully let her know that Tyrone did not own the club; Ray did. Tyrone just managed the club. Part of his rap to pick up chicks was to tell them that he owned the club and usually Ray didn't care. But this time he had to set the record straight.

"I've tried calling you, but you never returned my calls." "I know. I'm sorry;

I've been going through a lot."

"What, I can't hear you. Let's get out of here and go some- place quiet where we can talk."

Ray took her hand and guided her through the crowd. Everybody wanted to talk to him, but he kept moving. Once they were outside he spoke again.

"Damn, it's packed in there tonight. I get tired of that atmos- phere though, and you looked out of place. It's a nice night. Are you hungry?'

"Yeah. I could eat."

They walked down Broad Street, and Hope told him all she had been going through and dealing with since they met in Jamaica. Ray was a good listener and very sympathetic.

"Well, your husband is a fool, and it's good that you're rid of him. So that chapter in your life is over, and now it's time to move on. I'm so sorry about your mom. Nothing or no one will ever be able to fill that void in your life."

He stopped and turned to look her in the eyes.

"Now that I've found you again, I want to be a part of your life now. Will you let me?"

Hope didn't know what to say. This was so unexpected. But she was so comfortable with Ray. It was like they'd known each other for years.

"What about Sheryl? She told me you were her man. When she said her man's name was Ray, I never thought in a million years that it would be you. I never knew you were in this line of work. You never mentioned it. You told me about your real estate holdings and being on the board of the Boys and Girls Club. You never mentioned being a club owner or and coke dealer. This is a side of you I don't know."

"Well, for starters, I'm not Sheryl's man," Ray replied. "Sheryl doesn't want a man. Sheryl's man is cocaine. That's all she really cares about. All I am to her is a way to get high for free. As far as being a club owner and dealer, well, I didn't think that would be appealing to you, so I never mentioned it. That's not really who I am. That's what allowed me to gain capital to invest. Now it's just something that I do to allow others like Tyrone to make some money."

"Still. It doesn't feel right. I feel like I'm betraying her. I don't think—"

Ray grabbed her and kissed her passionately. Hope was breathless and speechless. This man made her feel safe, loved, and secure. She didn't say another word as he hailed down a cab and took her home to his place.

Ted was on his second glass of Remy when John arrived at the bar inside the downtown Sheraton. Ted's back was toward him so he snuck up behind him, kissed him on the neck, and whispered in his ear, "Hey, baby. I missed you."

Ted giggled like a schoolgirl as John sat beside him and ordered a Courvoisier.

"I missed you more, handsome. Look at you, Johnny!" Ted exclaimed as he rubbed John's inner thigh under the table. "Let's just skip dinner and go straight to the room."

After a passionate session of lovemaking, John and Ted lay in each other's arms, each in their own thoughts. John was thinking of a way to tell Ted that they can no longer continue seeing each other. He'd decided to stop this lifestyle while his daughters were there. He couldn't bear the thought of them finding out, and he couldn't bear the thought of telling them the truth. Not now. He knew Ted would take it hard, but this is how it had to be.

Ted was thinking how he was going to tell his wife the truth about his lifestyle. He knew she would be shocked, even though they'd only made love twice in their entire five years of marriage. She seemed content with just having a husband around to help around the house and take her out a few times each month. That was the extent of their relationship. They talked a lot, and Ted was a great listener. He listened to her talk out her problems with her work. He rubbed her feet, gave her massages, and cooked for her. She was content with their arrangement. Ted was content at first, but ever since he met Johnny, he'd become more and more resentful toward Anna. He wanted to spend all of his time with John. He knew that this summer would be difficult with the kids being here, but then again, these little getaways were rather excit- ing. He nuzzled closer under John's arm and fell asleep.

When Ted woke up John was gone. He found a note on the bed:

Dear Ted,

I'm sorry, but this has to be our last meeting. I can't continue to see you. I no longer want to live this lifestyle. I have two daughters that I have to raise, and they are looking to me to see how a man is supposed to treat them. I have to be an example of a real man for them.

I'm so sorry. I really do love you. I've never felt this way about anyone in my entire life. Maybe if we had met at a later time in my life things could be different. For now it must be like this. My daughters come first. Please understand and please don't call or come by the house.

Love always, Johnny

"You bastard!" Ted screamed. "I hate you! I hate you!" He rolled his body up into a ball and cried uncontrollably. When he finally stopped crying, he took a shower dressed and went home. He decided to continue with his plan to tell Anna the truth. She deserved to know the truth. And even though it was over between him and John, the truth of the matter was that he was gay. Period. *No more hiding and trying to be something I'm not*, he thought. *Yes, I'll take Anna out to a nice evening on the town and then tell her the truth.*

Hope woke up, leaned over to the nightstand, opened the drawer, pulled out a mirror with some lines of coke, and snorted two lines, one up each nostril. Then she lay back and let the drug take effect.

Ahhh. This is the life, she thought. It had been three months since Ray brought her to his home, and she never left. Ray took her shopping, and she got all new everything—from under- wear to shoes and accessories. She had a whole new wardrobe to accompany her whole new life. They spent two weeks in Jamaica and two weeks in Nassau. Ray was on business, and Hope was just chilling. She didn't even realize that she now had a $100- a-day cocaine habit because it was always so readily available. She didn't realize how much she was snorting. She woke up each morning to a snort and went to bed each night with a joint and a drink. During the days she shopped, ate, swam in the Olympic- size pool in Ray's backyard. Yes, she was living the life, but she missed her kids. They didn't seem to miss her as much though.

In August, Kennedy called and told her that she and Kamari decided to stay in Atlanta with their dad and go to school there in September. Kennedy's rationale was that she would be attend- ing Harriett Tubman University next year so she wanted to get familiar with the city and make some friends. Kamari had already made new friends and planned to join the pep squad. She would be entering the tenth grade and loved music, so Hope wasn't at all surprised at how excited she seemed about joining the band. She tried to sound happy for them because they really seemed happy about their decision. They had no idea how much it hurt Hope, and she wouldn't let them know. She just went along with their plans. She asked them if they need her to ship anything down to them, and their reply was, "No, Daddy bought us all new stuff."

She wiped the tears from her face and leaned over to take two more snorts when the house phone began ringing. Hope thought that was weird because no one ever called the house phone. Ray used his cell all the time, and Hope hadn't given anyone this number. She finally decided to answer it.

"Hello?" "Where's Ray?" "Sheryl?"

"Yes, it's me, bitch. Where's Ray? He doesn't want me coming to the house anymore and was supposed to meet me an hour ago with my package, and he ain't here yet."

"Listen, Sheryl. You don't have to call me names. Ray's not here. Did you try his cell phone?"

"Yeah, bitch! What? You think I'm stupid? That's the first thing I did, call his cell phone! Duh! Oh…wait…this him pull- ing up now." *Click.*

Sheryl had hung up the phone. *What the hell is her problem?* Hope thought as she prepared another line of coke. "She's been

acting funny ever since Hope and Ray had gotten together. Ray assured Hope that there was nothing going on between him and Sheryl, and he said that Sheryl was a lesbian. Hope had no idea of why Sheryl was acting so nasty toward her, and today she was totally out of line by calling her out her name. Hope made a men- tal note to address Sheryl the next time she saw her. She didn't have time right now. Today she was going to close on selling her mom's house. She was happy too. She realized that the time she lived there was very depressing for her. There were some unpleas- ant memories lingering there that she had put behind her a long time ago. Living there had only reminded her of her unpleasant childhood. Although she couldn't remember things in detail, she knew that the memories were not good. She remembered her grandmother taking her to live with her, and soon the memo- ries disappeared. Yes, the memories disappeared, but they mani- fested in her behavior as a teenager and young adult. She hated the memory of those years too and tried to make them disappear by marrying John. She thought that marrying a church boy would somehow redeem her from the sins of her past. She thought that emerging herself in the church and being a loyal and dutiful wife and mother would cleanse her from the sins of her youth.

Yes, she thought that she had finally made things right between her and God—until last year. She felt that last year God made himself perfectly clear to her. He did not care about her, and he did not hear her prayers. He didn't care that she tried her hardest to be a Christian wife and mother. She volunteered at her church and in her community. For fourteen years, she put her entire heart and soul into her marriage and into her children. She had even grown closer to her mother.

After years of feeling resentment toward her mother and dealing with feelings of abandonment, she and her mother had become best friends. Now? What? Her mother and new best friend were now dead—just gone. No warning. No explanation.

No good-bye. Just gone. Her husband had lied to her, cheated on her, cheated her out of money, and had now sent her divorce papers. She had two daughters whom she sacrificed her whole life for because she was determined that they would have the childhood that she always wanted and she vowed to do whatever it took to make that happen. And where were they now? Without a second thought about

Hope, they decided to live with their father. She had been abandoned again by the people whom she loved most in life. She picked up the mirror, prepared four lines of cocaine, and snorted two lines up each nose. She showered, dressed, and drove to the title company to settle the sale of her mother's house where she would collect a check for $125,000.

Hope went to the Outlets at Limerick and picked up some Christmas presents for her daughters. She really didn't know what to buy. Every time she called them they talked about all the things their father bought for them. She recalled that they never mentioned jewelry, so she bought Kennedy a sixteen-inch strand of pearls with matching dangling earrings. She bought both girls diamond tennis bracelets and matching earring, and each one got their birthstone jewelry, a ring, and matching earrings. She had the gifts wrapped, went to the post office, and had them shipped for next-day delivery with a note that said, "Don't open until Christmas." Feeling satisfied that they would be happy with the gifts; she made her way back to Ray's house.

"Come on, Anna, baby. Our reservation is for eight o'clock. It's seven thirty now." Ted was nervous but anxious to finally tell Anna the truth.

"Here I come, baby." Anna was excited about tonight. *Maybe after dinner we'll come home and make love*, she thought. Ted wasn't a very sexually active man, but when he got in the mood, he really got in the mood. Anna transformed herself into her sexy alter ego

Lola. That's what she called herself when she wore her blonde wig, red dress, and rubbed her Marc Jacobs Lola body creme all over her body and sprayed the perfume behind her ears, knees, and elbows. "Whatever Lola wants, Lola gets," she sang as she made her way down the stairs.

"Wow! You look great, babe!" Ted said. She really did look good. Ted knew she took extra care to look good for him tonight, and he felt bad.

"Let's go, babe."

As they waited for their dinner, they drank margaritas and talked about Anna's organization. She really was a fascinating woman. They had only been in the restaurant for about half an hour, and six people had come over to speak to her already. Outwardly he blushed each time she proudly introduced him as her husband, but on the inside he cringed. She had a lot going on. It's no wonder she didn't nag about sex; she didn't have time or energy half the time. As they ate dinner she asked him about his work and listened intently as he talked about his aspiration of becoming captain. His record as a police officer was unrivaled in his division. He had moved through the ranks pretty quickly, but the move from detective to captain wouldn't be easy. Unless the current captain dies or is promoted, he'll be in that posi- tion forever.

Just then the police commissioner walked past their table. He recognized Ted immediately. "Detective Anderson! Good to see you, sir! Your captain and I were just talking about you."

Just then Captain Turner walked up. "Hey, Ted. We were just talking about you. Man, you are one lucky son of a bitch! Oh, I'm sorry. Is this your beautiful wife? Hello, Mrs. Anderson. I'm Captain Turner."

"Not for long," the commissioner chimed in. "Evening, ma'am." He took Anna's hand and kissed it then turned to Ted.

"Ted, you obviously didn't watch the news tonight. Assistant Commissioner Howard held a press conference this evening announcing his resignation. The motherfucker is gay! He resigned before his shit came out in public. Apparently, he's been fucking around, and some of those faggots have been blackmailing him, so he decided it would be cheaper if he just resigned. And guess who's in line to take his place?"

He and Captain Turner shook their heads and laughed. Ted looked at them both in disbelief.

"Yup, you guessed it. I will announce Captain Turner as the new assistant commissioner tomorrow during a press conference. We just discussed calling on you to act as interim captain until your promotion becomes official. That is, if you want it."

Ted looked at Anna, who was screaming and clapping her hands. "God is so awesome!" she shouted! "Did you hear that, baby? We were just talking about your aspirations, and the Lord has placed them right at your table!"

"Of course I want it!" Ted exclaimed as he stood up and shook both their hands.

"Thank you. Thank you. You don't know how much this means to me. I won't disappoint you, sir."

"No, I don't believe you will," replied Captain Turner. "That stupid cocksucker made both our dreams come true."

"Yeah," Ted laughed halfheartedly. "Stupid cocksucker!"

John hadn't heard from Brad in weeks. The projects were on schedule and running smoothly. The whole operation was running like a well-oiled machine. John really didn't have much to do at work other than review the project manager's reports. He was happy about it because it gave him time to spend with his daughters. Christmas was just a few weeks away, and they were so excited. They were like kids again, and John loved it. He missed a lot of their childhood because he was so busy working and doing his thing. Now he was just as excited as they were. Terry had moved in, and it felt like he had a family. Things were going really well. Hope hadn't objected to the terms of the divorce and accepted his new offer of $4,000 monthly alimony. Terry and the girls were out for the evening shopping for Christmas decorations and gifts. Life was good. But still, he couldn't understand why Brad hadn't returned his calls for two weeks now. He looked at the mail that had piled up on the dining room table. He hadn't opened mail in weeks. He poured himself a glass of Courvoisier, sat down, and began going through the mail. There was an envelope from the law offices of Williams and Foster. At first John thought it was Hope's lawyer, and then he remembered that Williams and Foster represented the company's legal affairs.

Damn. I hope we're not being sued, John thought as he opened the letter. It read,

> Dear Mr. Daroff:
>
> Please be advised that effective January 1, 2003, your employment with J. D. Industries LLC will terminate. Attached you will find a generous severance package that includes two years' severance pay and the option to stay in the company-owned penthouse rent free for two years.
>
> J. D. Industries LLC appreciates your years of loyal service and wishes you the best in your future endeavors.

"What the fuck! That's *my* fucking company! They gonna fire *me*?"

He picked up the phone and dialed Brad's number again. This time he answered.

"Hello?"

"Brad? What's up, man? I've been calling you for two weeks, and today I get a letter saying that my employment with my own company will be terminated at the beginning of the new year? What the fuck is going on, man? I thought we had an agreement?"

"John, man I'm sorry, I've been out of town. Listen, the board has decided not to go through with giving you any percentage of ownership in the company. This decision was based on your past performance at your other company. Your position is no longer needed. We decided to eliminate it because there is no real func- tion. We felt we were generous in giving you two years' salary and two years rent free. That gives you a pretty nest egg for a new beginning."

John was speechless. He just hung up the phone. He couldn't believe what was happening. He could kick himself for not get- ting the agreement in writing. He couldn't even take them to court—or could he? Sometimes a verbal agreement is just as con- tractual as a written agreement. He'd have to consult his attorney. He poured himself another drink and began thinking about Ted. He missed Ted. He could use the comfort of his embrace right now. Terry was fine for family appearances, and she liked anal sex and gave good head, but Ted was John's lover. They had created a bond that John couldn't shake. It had been five months since their last rendezvous. Ted hadn't called, and they hadn't seen each other since then. He decided to call Ted, but his phone went straight to voice mail. Just then the girls and Terry came through the door loaded down with bags. They had no doubt spent a small fortune.

"Hey, Daddy! It's beginning to look a lot like Christmas!" Kamari exclaimed. She looked so happy. She had begun to open up to John over the past five months. She ran over and gave John a big hug.

"We decided to go with a color scheme of red and gold," she said as she began pulling out the decorations to show him.

"Yes, Daddy, Remember when we were little our Christmas tree was red and

gold and it spun around in circles and play
'Silent Night'? We loved that tree!" Kennedy chimed in.

"Yes. We're gonna make this place into a Christmas wonder- land!" Terry added.

John looked at the three smiling faces, and all he could do was join in the merriment. He wouldn't allow the new state of affairs to put a damper on his family's happiness.

"Well, let's get started!" he said as he popped in the Jackson 5
Christmas CD.

When Hope got back to Ray's house, he was in the den on the phone.

"Man. That sounds like a real good deal—$200,000 will get me $500,000? That's 150 percent profit. Can't beat that. Yeah, I got about $100,000." He looked up as Hope walked in. She walked over and kissed him on the cheek. She hadn't told him about selling her mom's house. He'd been so busy lately. He had taken such good care of her for the past six months, and she was so grateful. No man had ever taken care of her like he had. She wanted to surprise him with something. Do something special to show her appreciation. She sat down and listened to the rest of his conversation.

"Maybe I can get an investor or two to come in with me on the deal. You say the product is pure, right? Okay. I'll get back to you in a week. Talk to you then."

"Hey, baby! Wow, you look great! You look like you're glow- ing… You not pregnant, are you?"

"No," Hope laughed. "I'm just happy and so grateful to have you in my life, baby."

Ray grabbed her and kissed her. He had never felt like this about a woman. Most of the woman he knew were only out for his money or drugs or both. Hope never asked for or expected anything. That's why she got everything. She deserved it. She was a good woman. He knew that when he first saw her on the plane going to the Bahamas a few years ago. He was shocked when she showed up at his club—and with Sheryl at that. When he found out that her husband left her and that she and Sheryl were old friends, he stepped right in. He kept her away from Sheryl too. She was bad news. Truth be told, Sheryl probably wanted Hope for herself. Hope had no idea that Sheryl was even a lesbian. He wanted to shield Hope from the ugliness of his world but at the same time wanted her to be a part of his world.

Hope interrupted his thoughts. "I want to take you out tonight. Let's rent a limo and drive to New York and have dinner of the rooftop of the Waldorf Astoria. My treat."

"Wow. What'd you do? Hit the number? Your treat? I'm in." They rode to New York in a white stretch limo, drinking champagne and nibbling on peanuts and pretzels.

"Ray, if you could do anything you wanted, what would you do?"

Ray thought about that. When he was a kid he liked to draw. He was pretty good at it too. He hadn't drawn anything in years.

"I'd want to be an artist. Just have a house in the mountains or by the beach, with you and our kids. I would just paint pictures. That's what I'd want to do if I could. What about you, babe? What would you do?"

Hope had always wanted to be a lawyer. She still wanted to be one. "I'd go to law school and start my own private law practice."

"So, babe. If we could make about two million dollars, we could buy a house in the mountains and send you to law school.

I could get out of the game. Sell the club. We could be set up for a nice, little comfortable lifestyle."

They arrived at the restaurant, ordered dinner, and ate in silence. Each in their own thoughts. On the way home Hope told Ray about the house.

"Guess what I did today?" "What, babe?"

"I sold my mother's house and got $125,000 profit. Now, I overheard your conversation and understand that you need $100,000 investor. I want to be that investor, baby. I want to help you. You've been so good to me; I want to return the favor."

Ray looked her in the eyes. He was filled with so much love for her at that moment that a tear rolled down his cheek. Hope kissed it, then him. They made love during the entire ride home.

Sheryl sat in the cell shivering as the drugs wore off. The cops had picked her up as she was about to make a purchase for Ray. Ten grand down the drain. He was gonna be real pissed off about this shit. She blew her nose again. The guard came and unlocked her cell door. "Evans. Come with me." He led her to a room where two detectives were seated.

"Listen, Evans. We know you are just a pawn, and we don't want you. We want your boss, Raymond Montgomery. We know he's in the game big. Now, if you help us get him, you can go scot free."

Sheryl didn't think twice before agreeing to that offer. This would be her chance to get him back for taking Hope away from her.

"What do you want me to do?" she asked.

Ted settled into his office and position as captain very easily. The officers in his precinct were happy for him, and everyone was very cooperative helping to make the transition run smoothly. He always knew the climate of homophobia within the police district and had seen officers who displayed homosexual tendencies tormented, beaten, and dehumanized to a point where they left the force. He'd always been careful not to show any signs at work. He almost gave everything up. If he had gone through with his plan to tell Anna the truth, he would probably have lost everything, including his job. Now he was having sex with his wife on a regular basis—always doggy style. But he missed and longed for John bad. John had called his cell phone several times, but Ted never answered, and John never left a message. Ted hadn't been with another man since John. He didn't even have the yearning to go out and peruse the bars or bathhouses looking for men either. He kept busy working and was enjoying being married. Still, he knew that if he saw John again, those old feelings would emerge, so he vowed to stay away from John. He hurt him bad. How could he just leave him with a dear John letter? How ironic was that. But it all worked out.

Ted was satisfied. He was content in his new lifestyle. Christmas was just a few days away, and he bought Anna the blue fox jacket he saw her looking at in the window of Zinman Furs. She was a damn good woman, and Ted wanted to make up for neglecting her for so long. Fuck a John Daroff.

John couldn't find an artificial Christmas tree that played "Silent Night," so they agreed to purchase a real tree. It was Christmas Eve, and he helped the girls decorate the tree. Their first Christmas Eve in Atlanta was going to be special. They had invited a bunch of their friends over, and Terry made cookies, and they were ordering pizzas and hot wings. John was happy because they were happy, but he sure missed Ted.

After the party got started, he decided to go for a drive. Before he realized it, he was on Ted's block. He pulled across the street at the top of the hill. He had a good view of the house from there. He sat looking at the house and reminiscing when Ted pulled into the driveway. John watched him as he took wrapped pack- ages out of his trunk and took them into the house. John decided to go and talk to him. He walked up the driveway and rang the bell. Ted opened the door.

"Merry Chri—" He stopped midsentence. "John?" "Hi, Ted. Merry

Christmas. May I come in?"

Ted was still in shock as he stepped aside and allowed John to come in. He shut the door and turned around, and John grabbed him, and they embraced and began kissing passionately. Ted led John down to the back room in the basement. He knew Anna wouldn't be home for at least another hour or two. Her organiza- tion was out singing Christmas carols and taking toys to women's shelters. She never came in through the basement anyway, so if she did come in, they'd hear her and have time to stop. His body was on fire, and he wanted John right at the moment. They spoke no words but went straight to fucking. After a fierce, quick, and passionate fuck they looked up, and Anna was standing in the doorway of the room looking through tears with shock and dis- belief on her face.

"Anna! What…how…"

She turned to run but tripped over the bags she was sneaking in—bags full of gifts for her husband. Ted pulled up his pants and ran over to help her.

"Anna, let me explain."

"Explain what?" she screamed. "Explain that you're a fucking faggot? I just watched you allow another man to put his dick up your ass. What is it that you think you can explain to me, Ted?"

She got up, rant to their bedroom, and started throwing some clothes into a suitcase. Ted came in right behind her.

"Anna, wait! Please. Don't leave like this. We need to talk. I wanted to tell you."

"When, Ted? When were you ever going to tell me?" she screamed hysterically. "I doubt that you ever would have told me or anyone else, seeing how this would affect your position at the Police Department. Just what do you think will happen when they find out that their new highly esteemed captain is a big fag- got just like the former assistant commissioner? How ironic is that? The only reason you got to be captain is because the fag- got commissioner resigned, and now they're gonna find out that you're a faggot too!"

She grabbed her suitcase and started down the hallway. "Anna! Don't do this!

Please! We can work it out," Ted said as he ran after her and grabber her arm just before she started down the steps.

She pulled away from him. "Don't you touch me! Get your punk-bitch ass away from me!" She grabbed her suitcase and swung around to hit him, lost her balance, and fell down the steps. John was at the bottom of the steps listening the entire time. He walked over to Anna's motionless body and felt her neck for a pulse.

"She's alive. Man, I'm so sorry. I never wanted this to happen. I didn't know you made captain! Congratulations! That's what you've always wanted."

"Yeah. All that's about to change because she's gonna go tell every- and anybody who will listen. I can kiss my career good-bye."

"Well, we can't let that happen, can we?" John said as he picked up Anna's suitcase. "Here, take this back upstairs, unpack it, and put it where it belongs."

"Why? What are you going to do, John?"

"You want to keep your career, don't you? You want to keep your life right? I have a plan. Just trust me and do what I say."

While Ted put Anna's clothes back, John opened some can- dles that were in one of the bags Anna bought home. *Looks like she was planning a romantic evening*, he thought as he laid a new negligee out on the bed and lit all the candles.

"Go get in your car and drive to the Vortex. I'll meet you there in about an hour."

Ted looked worried. "What are you going to do, John?" he asked slowly, but he didn't really want to know.

"I'm gonna take care of everything, baby. Don't worry. I'm gonna make sure everything is okay. Now, I'll meet you in about an hour."

Ted went to the bathroom, splashed some water on his face, and fixed his clothes. Then he went outside, got into his car, and drove off.

John lit the candles and let them burn for about a half hour before knocking two of them onto the floor. He watched as the flame caught the edge of the bedspread and started to burn up the bed. He made his way downstairs, stopped at Anna's body, and banged her head against the floor twice to make sure she remained unconscious. He made the scene look like Anna saw the fire, tried to get out of the house, ran downstairs, and fell, knocking herself unconscious. He left out the basement and walked across the street and up the hill where he'd parked his car. He got in his car and sat, watching as the house went up in flames. He never went to the bar to meet Ted. Instead he drove

home and joined in the festivities with Terry and his children—
as if nothing ever happened.

Hope woke with a start. She sat straight up. Something hit her in the gut. She wanted her children to come home.

"Good morning, babe. Merry Christmas," Ray said as he kissed her. "What's wrong? Did you have a bad dream?"

"I need to get a house and get my kids back. I want them back home with me, Ray. Something just doesn't feel right. I gotta get my kids back." She started crying.

"Okay. Okay. We can do that. Do they want to come back? I thought they were happy staying with their father."

"I don't care what *they* want. They need to come back here with me. That's all I know."

Ray held her and rocked her back to sleep. Then he got up, made breakfast and brought her in a tray with cantaloupe, eggs, pancakes, turkey sausage, tea, and orange juice. They ate in bed together before going downstairs to open their gifts. There was only one small box under the tree for Hope. There were two large boxes and one small box for Ray. She made him open his gifts first. He was ecstatic over his new leather jacket, two tailor-made shirts, and a pair of cufflinks with his initials separated by one- carat diamonds on each one. He grabbed the small box and gave it to Hope. She opened it to find a two-carat ruby ring surrounded by diamond baguettes. Ray got down on one knee.

"Baby, I've never felt like this about anyone in my entire life. I can't imagine living without you. Everything I do, I do with you in mind. There is no future for me without you. I bought you a ruby ring instead of a diamond because I remember reading in the Bible a long time ago that a good woman is worth more than rubies. I know you're a good woman. I love you. Will you be my wife?"

Hope was crying like a baby but managed to say, "Yes. Yes. *Yes*!" He put the ring on her finger, and they lay on the floor in front of the Christmas tree in silence. Ray thinking how happy he was and how once they did this last deal, they would be set, and he would get out of the game for good. Hope was thinking how it was almost noon, and her children hadn't called her yet. After about fifteen minutes, she decided to call them. John answered the phone. He saw on the caller ID that it was Hope.

"Hello?"

"Hello? John? This is Hope. Merry Christmas."

He didn't respond.

"Are the girls up yet."

"Are they up? They're up and out, Hope. They went to Christmas brunch at Terry's cousin's house. You're a little late calling, don't you think? Or were you too busy getting high with your boyfriend?"

He'd heard all about Hope and her new man, Ray the Drug Dealer. Philly was a small town, and people loved to talk.

"Well, I was waiting for them to call me. I thought they'd call after opening the gifts I sent. They did get the gifts, didn't they?" She totally ignored his comment about Ray.

"Oh, I did see a slip from the post office that there were pack- ages to be picked up. I forgot all about it. So, no, they didn't get your gifts. They're still at the post office."

Hope was speechless.

"Listen, Hope, I don't want you calling my house. Kamari and Kennedy both have cell phones now. That was one of their gifts from me. I'll have them call you, and when you want to talk to

them, you call their cell phones. Oh, and by the way, I'm rescind- ing my alimony offer, and I'm filing for full custody of the girls. In light of your present living situation, you're not fit to be the custodial parent, and I'm not paying alimony to you and your drug-dealer boyfriend." *Click.*

Hope stared at the phone and began crying uncontrollably. Ray came into the kitchen, took the phone out of her hand, and hung it up. He'd been listening from the living room phone. He heard the entire conversation. He didn't know what to say. He felt terrible after watching the way she woke up with a conviction that the girls needed to come back home with her. He had already started thinking of purchasing a house for her and her kids.

"Tomorrow we go looking at houses. By January we'll have you in a house, and I want you to go back to school. You keep say- ing you want to be a lawyer. Well, now is the time to start making that happen. I want you to look into going back and getting your bachelor's and enrolling into law school. Once the courts see you doing things to better yourself, they will not take any child from their mother. I guarantee that."

"B-b-b-but th-they didn't even call me, Ray. They didn't even call," she cried. "They didn't call to say 'Merry Christmas, Mommy' or even to say hi. I haven't heard from them in weeks. I've been leaving messages, but no doubt John erased them and never told them that I called. They must hate me. They're old enough now to decide which parent they want to live with, and I'm sure he's poisoned them against me. They won't want to live with me, Ray."

Ray knew she was right. He didn't want to make her feel any worse than she already did.

"Well, that remains to be seen. Just wait and see what they say. Hopefully they will call you on their own because we both know John won't bother telling them that you called."

"Why does he hate me so much, Ray? I gave him everything. I never contested anything—never asked him for anything. After my mom died I needed time to get myself together. That's why I allowed them to go stay with him for the summer. I thought he was being kind and helpful, but all the while he just wanted to turn them against me. He knows I love my girls. My entire life revolved around them. And now…" She just broke down at that point, falling to her knees with her head in her hands crying. Not knowing what to say, Ray just knelt down and held her.

"Stupid bitch," John said as he sat down and turned on the TV. "She gets nothing. She wants to be a drug dealer's girlfriend now? You can never take a bitch out of the ghetto. I took that bitch places she'd never been. Seen places she'd never seen. Had her rubbing elbows with politicians, judges, lawyers—rich people with class. And what does she do? Go back to drugs. Back to that thug life. Well, she wasn't taking the girls with her. No, they'll be better off here with me."

He switched the channel to the local news. The breaking news story was about the wife of a local police captain killed in a house fire on Christmas Eve. The reporter was interviewing some lady from Anna's organization.

"We spent the entire day together yesterday. This is all so very hard to take in. We went last-minute shopping. She was plan- ning a romantic night for her husband and had purchased some scented candles and lingerie. After we distributed toys to the Women and Children's Shelter, she said she was going home the get ready for an evening with her husband. She didn't even join us to go sing Christmas carols. All she talked about was getting home before her husband to get some romantic ambiance going on. She was so happy. I can't believe she's gone."

The cameral came back to the reporter.

"Fire authorities say that the fire was started in the bedroom where numerous candles were lit. Looks like a night planned for romance turned into a roaring inferno."

John flicked the remote again. The story was being covered on all the local channels. One station reported that the husband was too distraught and refused to be interviewed.

Well, John thought. *Some things have to be done for the greater good.* He poured himself a cognac and lifted his glass in a toasting gesture. "Here's to Anna Anderson and Peter Hamilton. Never try to disclose the brotherhood." He drank with no remorse.

He thought about what today represented. The birth of the Messiah Jesus the Christ. He thought about that Christmas Eve many, many years ago when he was just a boy. His mother had to work late for the white family who employed her as their maid. They were having guests over. His mother asked Deacon Frye to watch after John after the evening Christmas play at church. Deacon Frye looked after him all right. That night was the first of many nights that Deacon Frye "looked after him" while his mother worked late. His mother had no idea of what the good deacon did to him. He tried to tell his mother once, but she wasn't hearing any of it. She always reminded John how good the deacon was to them. He bought him things, took him places, and they shared a very "special bond" as Deacon Frye often reminded him. He swore John to secrecy, assuring him that this type of thing was natural and happened to all little boys. It had happened to Deacon Frye too when he was about John's age.

"It's just the way things are," Deacon Frye would tell John. After a while, John believed it was true. He learned that many of the other little boys who attended church with him also had "special bonds" with other deacons, the choir director, and other men in the church. That Christmas Eve was when he stopped

believing. He stopped believing in Santa Claus, and he stopped believing in Jesus Christ. He continued to play church, though, just like the older men. He went to service faithfully, sang and shouted, and continued having special bonds with important men in the church. He learned at a young age that these spe- cial bonds came with special rewards. He liked the rewards and learned to like the special bonds. Church had become a place where he went to meet influential people, to develop bonds with different men, to get special rewards, and to make important con- nections. Church had become a place for all of those things, but not a place where he found Jesus or God. He had abandoned that notion as a young boy.

Hope was new to church life, and she bought into the notion that the church was where the Holy Spirit dwelt and all that crap. When they first got married he earnestly tried to seek the Lord and asked for forgiveness and became an active member. But soon he saw and got caught up in the spirit—the spirit of lies, deceptions, and special bonds.

Most of these men had wives and families and held high posi- tions in church and in the society. Some wives knew and were what was referred to as "beards." A beard is a woman who know- ingly marries a homosexual man to keep up appearances. She is willing to do this in return for money and prominence in society. He soon became a part of the club, but Hope was naive and never suspected a thing. He had given up believing in the God that he learned about as a boy a long time ago. He saw no evidence of this God in church. He saw no evidence of this Jesus Christ who loved the world so much that he died for all the sins of the whole world. He didn't buy that crap anymore. The theme of this life is "Get rich or die trying." Whatever it takes, just do it. And that's how John vowed to live.

Ted was in a complete state of shock. He knew John was planning something terrible, but this? He burnt down Ted's whole house— his whole life—along with his wife. He stood outside looking at the charred wood, furniture, pictures, tools, art—everything. When they bought Anna out in a body bag, he lost it. A bunch of guys from his precinct were there, along with the assistant commissioner, his former boss. They held on to Ted as he tried to get to the body bag. He was truly hysterical.

He couldn't believe she was dead. He really did love her and never imagined anything like this happening. He was wrought with despair, but most of all it was guilt. He knew her death was his fault, and he didn't think he would ever get over that.

He sat in the bar at the Vortex for two and a half hours wait- ing for John. He called once, and the phone went straight to voice mail. He ended up drinking with a few guys from his precinct—a few of whom were there trying to hold him together. These guys spent most of their holidays at the bar because their marriages had failed. That was the story of a lot of cops—failed marriages. The guys had no idea Ted was gay. They had all been in attend- ance at his wedding just five years ago. Last night they teased him about still being in the honeymoon stage, saying they will gave him two more years before the proverbial seven-year itch kicked in.

After six shots of tequila he was laughing and joking right along with them. When Jack suggested Ted get home to his wife while he still had one, he agreed, but was in no shape to drive. Jack drove him home, and they could smell and see the smoke blocks away. Ted knew something terrible had happened and began to sober up. As they got close to his block, all he could see was fire engines and ambulances blocking the way to his street. He jumped out of Jack's car and ran toward his house with Jack close behind. His worst fear was recognized when he saw that it

was his house that was burning. He tried to get closer, but the police and firemen blocked him.

"that's my house that's burning!" he screamed.

"I'm very sorry, sir, but I can't let you go any farther. We don't want anyone else getting hurt."

"Anyone else? What do you mean anyone else? Where's my wife? Has anybody seen my wife?"

"Sir, please step back while they get the fire under control." "Come on, Ted,"

Jack said. "Let's just wait—and pray."

So here he was now—watching them carry his wife away in a body bag. His mind and body were riddled with guilt so much so that he began to throw up. He ended up in the hospital for dehydration. He couldn't hold anything down. He still hadn't heard from John. The visitors flowed through his room from the time visiting hours started until the time they ended. His fellow police officers, members from Anna's church, and her work had filled his room with flowers and fruit baskets. He still couldn't keep anything down and had IV in both arms: one for nutrition and one for potassium. He'd had offers from three of Anna's girl- friends from church to bunk at their homes. The commissioner already had gotten him a place at Korman Suites. He'd also been the one to contact his insurance company. Anna's sister, Doreen, came from LA and was making the funeral arrangements. She hadn't been to see Ted, and he wasn't a bit surprised. They never did hit it off. He was glad she was here to take care of the funeral arrangements though. He wouldn't have been able to handle that. The night before he was released, he was awakened in the mid- dle of the night by someone kissing him. He woke to find John standing over him.

"Hey, baby. I'm sorry I didn't show up at the Vortex or return your calls. I decided it would be better to distance ourselves, just

to be on the safe side. I just want you to know that I'm still here, and I still love you."

He was gone before Ted could utter a word. When he woke the next morning he didn't know if he'd dreamed the whole scene or if it was real. When he got to his place a Korman Suites and found two dozen yellow roses among all the other flowers, he knew he hadn't dreamed it at all. John was the only person who had ever bought him yellow roses.

It turned out that Anna had all her paperwork in order: liv- ing will, last will and testament, power of attorney, etc. Her sister had all power of attorneys and was executor of her estate, which was pretty vast. Anna was cremated according to her wishes, which was fitting because her body was burned to a char in the fire anyway. Doreen did a good job planning and implement- ing the memorial service too. Ted did nothing except wallow in his guilt—a guilt that everyone else mistook for mournful grief. Anna left everything to her closest relative—her sister, Doreen.

But Ted was the beneficiary of her one-million-dollar life insurance policy. When he heard that, he cried some more. The insurance company didn't question him or the circumstances of Anna's death. They processed the payment immediately. Their house was insured for $1.5 million. Anna was insistent on mak- ing sure that if anything happened to their ho

me that they would be able to start over with monetary ease. Financially Ted was set for life. A life that would be full of guilt and torment.

The New Year started off bright. Ray came through for Hope once again. By mid-January she was in a three-bedroom house in Cheltenham Township. He wanted here to get a place there because they had a good school system. She had enrolled in Beaver College and was scheduled to start classes in two weeks. She was

only twenty-six credits away from obtaining her bachelor's degree. She decided to major in business administration and specialize in business law.

The girls did call her on Christmas night. Their father finally got around to telling them about the gifts at the post office and her phone call to them earlier that day. It wasn't that they hadn't thought about her, but they were only afraid that Hope was too busy and had forgotten about them. Hope assured them that nothing could be farther from the truth. They picked their gifts up the next day and loved them. They sent Hope a beauti- ful silk scarf and broach. Now that they had cell phones, they called at least twice a week. They were enjoying life in Atlanta but agreed to come back to Philly and spend spring break with her. Hope still had a very uneasy feeling about them being in Atlanta with John, but they sounded so happy—especially Kamari. She seemed to have come out of her shell. She guessed John couldn't be all that bad.

Yes, this year looked promising. One of her New Year's resolu- tions was to give up cocaine, and so far she'd stuck to it. She still smoked weed though and went out on the back deck to light one up as she waited for her new bedroom and living room sets to be delivered.

She also bought herself a new wardrobe when she realized that almost her entire wardrobe was black. She remembered André telling her how the color of your clothes symbolized how you felt. Black was a color or protection; it created an air of mys- tery. She was covering her feelings. She never mourned the loss of her mother, her home, her business, or her children. She covered it all with her black clothing. She decided to spice up her black with some hunter-green, winter-white, red, and blue pieces from a boutique she found downtown. She didn't want to go to school wearing black every day.

Ray didn't move in with her. He wanted her to look good in the eyes of the court. He put the deed in her name, but he made the mortgage payments. She gave him $100,000 to invest in the package deal. After buying new furniture, gifts for the girls, and books for the semester, she only had $5,700 in her bank account. She wasn't worried though. Ray was picking up the package today. He said the turnover time would be about a month, and then she'd be up $250,000. She put in the new Mary J. Blige CD, lit a joint, and began singing, "I wouldn't change my life, my life's just fine." She was interrupted by the phone ringing.

"Hello?"

"Hope. It's Ray. I got locked up. I'm at the Delaware County Prison. Go to my house and get my lawyer's card out of my desk drawer. His name is Rubenstein. Jack Rubenstein. Tell him I'm in the Delaware County Prison and I need him to get here immediately."

"Huh? Oh no! Are you okay. What happened?"

"It was a set up. The package deal was a set up. I don't know who set me up, but when I find out…just get to house and call the lawyer."

"Okay. What—" He hung up before Hope could complete her question. She had lots of questions.

Her high was completely blown. And she definitely wasn't feeling Mary J. anymore. She grabbed her keys and purse and drove to Ray's house and called the lawyer. Jack Rubenstein picked her up from Ray's, and they drove to the prison together. They waited for over three hours before being allowed to see Ray, and even then, only the lawyer was allowed to speak with him. After almost two more hours, Jack came out. He told her that because it was Friday, Ray wouldn't have a bail hearing until Monday and would have to stay in jail until then. During the ride home he explained that Ray had attempted to purchase three kilos of cocaine from a federal agent. *Federal agent*. He explained the seriousness of the crime and told her that Ray would most probably do some time. "He was trying to purchase a very large quantity and from the feds. There's really no way around this."

When Hope got home, she sat on the living room floor in the dark for a long time. Then she just started sobbing when she realized she'd missed her furniture delivery. Not that any of that mattered at this point. She had $5,700 to her name. Ray paid her mortgage up for a year. She was thankful for that. She hadn't snorted any coke in about a month, but she wanted some now. Instead, she lit up a joint and sat in the dark.

The ringing phone woke her up the next morning. It was Tyrone, the manager from Ray's club.

"Hope? Damn, girl. I've been calling all morning. You behind the eight ball?"

"Yes, yes, I'm okay. I was just sleeping."

"Well, it's one o'clock in the afternoon. Listen, I'm trying to get some money together for Ray's bail. I know he has some cash stashed in the safe in his house. Do you have the combination?"

"No, no, I don't know anything about that. I think he used all the money he had for the package. I don't think there's any money left."

"Wow. Okay. Don't worry about it. I'll handle it. Are you okay? Do you need anything?"

"No. I'm fine."

"Okay. Well, call me if you need anything."

Tyrone passed the cocaine-lined mirror over to Sheryl.

"She's on edge. We don't have to worry about her. Good job, Sheryl. Now the cops will stay off our backs and concentrate on

Ray. I'll make sure Hope is taken care of. She's gonna need some- body to take care of her now."

Hope didn't know what day it was or how long she'd been sleep. She looked over at the table beside her bed, and there were three fat joints rolled. She remembered rolling them. There was a half a joint in the ashtray. She lit it up and inhaled deeply. It was dark outside, and she heard her stomach growling. She couldn't remember the last time she ate. She went into the kitchen to see what she had to eat. To her surprise there was a bowl of fresh fruit on the table: apples, pears, and oranges. In the refrigerator there were grapes and strawberries, milk, orange juice, and some fried chicken in a Pathmark bag. She wondered who bought this food. She didn't remember anyone being here. She grabbed an apple, washed it, and devoured it. Then she ate a pear and drank a glass of orange juice. She felt refreshed and grabbed a drumstick and ate it too. Then she went back to her room, lit up another joint, and began to remember her situation. Ray was in prison, and her mom was dead. She hadn't heard from her girls in a while. The thought of that depressed her even more. She didn't know or care what day it was. She went back to sleep.

The smell of bacon woke her up the next morning. She went to the kitchen and found Tyrone there cooking bacon, pancakes, and eggs.

"Good morning, Miss Hope," he said without turning to look at her. He could smell her from where he was standing.

"Why don't you go take a shower and put on some clean clothes while I finish making breakfast?"

Hope looked down at her clothes. As she made her way back upstairs to the bathroom, she tried to remember the last time she showered. The last time she was in this state of mind was when she found out about the dirty, underhanded deal John did with the company. Her cousin, Patty, was the one who took care of her then. She missed her cousin. She missed her kids. Most of all she missed her mom. Now with Ray locked up and all her money gone, she didn't know what she was going to do. She let the water from the shower run down her hair and face and began to cry. As she started to cry, she realized that—as crazy as it was—she missed John. She didn't want to cry; she was strong. She pulled herself together and washed up. When she walked back into her bedroom, she realized what a mess it was. Her box spring and mattress were still on the floor because she still didn't get her bedroom set. There were apple and pear cores and chicken bones on the floor along with a glass and an empty orange juice carton. She opened one of the bins where her clothes were still packed, pulled out a pair of jeans and a sweatshirt, put them on, and went downstairs.

Tyrone had the small kitchen table set with a beautiful orchid in the center. She sat down as he placed a plate of pancakes, eggs, and bacon in front of her. Hope was famished! She put a forkful of pancakes, eggs, and bacon in her mouth all at the same time.

"You look *and smell* much better!" He laughed as he placed a glass of orange juice in front of her.

"When's the last time you ate food?"

"I don't know. Evidently I got up and ate apples, pears, and chicken at some point. Was it you who bought that food here for me? What day is it?"

"Yes, it was me, and today is Sunday."

"Oh. It feels like so much time has gone by. So tomorrow is
Ray's bail hearing. Were you able to get any money together?"

"Hope, Ray's bail hearing was last week. You've been asleep for a week. I got the keys to your place from Ray's house. There wasn't enough money in his safe to bail him out, so he's gonna be in prison until his trial comes up in about six to nine months."

Hope slowed down eating, but she didn't stop. The food was delicious, and she was starving. She ate the rest of her breakfast in silence. She didn't even notice that Tyrone had left the kitchen. After she finished, she went into the living room and picked up the stack of mail that had piled up. There was a welcome packet from the post office and Verizon, circulars, fliers, and two enve- lopes from lawyers. One envelope was from a law firm in Atlanta and one from a local attorney. She opened the envelope from Atlanta first. It was divorce papers that not only removed the original agreement of spousal support, but now John was also seeking child support for Kennedy and Kamari! The amount he was asking for was $3,000 per month—a number they came up with based on how much money she made when they had the company. The letter said that the courts would base the amount of child support requested on her "potential income." She tossed that aside and opened the other letter from the local attorney. This letter informed her that she was being sued by her mother's son Donté for selling their mother's house without his consent. He was seeking half the money from the settlement. Hope tossed the mail back onto the mantle and went back to her bedroom.

Tyrone had cleaned up the room and changed the sheets on her mattress. She could hear water running in the bathroom, but she didn't even have the strength to go and thank him. All she could do was crawl back onto the mattress on the floor and pull the covers over her head. She vaguely heard Tyrone say some- thing about the furniture being delivered tomorrow before she drifted off the sleep again.

"Hope, wake up. Wake up, Hope."

Hope heard Tyrone's voice as she started to come out of her sleep. She could feel the sunlight beaming through the window.

She pulled the covers back over her head and rolled over onto her stomach.

"Come on, Hope. You have to get up. You've been sleep for over a week. The delivery truck will be here in an hour. You need to get up and get dressed and get back to living," Tyrone said as he pulled the covers off her. He had four lines of cocaine on a mirror for her to help her get moving.

"Here. Take a tote."

Hope looked at the white powder on the glass. It had been at least two months since she'd had any coke in her system. Her New Year's resolution was to stop snorting. Well, that was when the New Year looked bright and promising. Now everything was dark and black, and those four little white lines shimmering on the glass were calling her name. She took the rolled-up bill, snorted the first line up her right nostril, and followed up with another line up her right one. She immediately felt the familiar rush and sense of euphoria.

Tyrone could see that she was coming around.

"I'll go downstairs and make some coffee. Get in the shower and get dressed.

Hope watched him walk out the door and wondered why he was being so nice to her. She knew that he'd liked her, but he barely said two words to her after she left the club with Ray that night. Now here he was, making sure she ate, bathed, and trying to help her get back to the business of living. She got up, show- ered, dressed, and finished off the two lines of coke that was left on the mirror. The doorbell rang, and she heard Tyrone talking to the delivery guy telling them where to put each piece of the living room set. He told them to bring in the bedroom set first and then yelled up the stairs to tell Hope they were coming up. Hope quickly took the mirror and put it in the bathroom cabinet.

After about two hours all the furniture was in place. Hope sipped on her cup of coffee as she stood looking at her new liv- ing and dining room sets. They looked really nice. She had opted for the cherrywood dining room table and cherrywood finish on her sofa and love seat with green and burgundy paisley pillows and cushions. Tyron sat down at the dining room table with the pile of mail in front of him. He pulled out a bag of coke, took a tote, then offered it to Hope. She sat down at the table and took a few totes.

"I went through your mail. You can't just sleep this shit away, Hope. You're gonna have to deal with the shit. You got your hus- band suing you for child support and your brother suing you for selling your mom's house. You have about five grand in your bank account. Ray's going to be away for at least ten years. Let me take care of you, baby. You know I've always had a thing for you. Let me help you now. Okay?"

Hope looked Tyrone in straight in the eyes. She could see sin- cerity there. She didn't really know him that well, but he seemed to genuinely care about her. She sure needed someone to care about her, and she needed someone to take care of her too. She finally nodded yes as she took two more totes of cocaine.

Ray was surprised when the guard came to get him. He was told he had a visitor. He hoped it was Hope. He hadn't seen or heard from her since he'd been locked up. Her cell phone number had been changed, and she hadn't responded to any of his letters. When he got to the visitor's area he saw Sheryl waiting at a table—alone.

"Hey, Ray! You look well. How you making out, baby?"

"As well as can be expected. What you doin' here? How's Hope? What's up with her?"

"Man, your girl hooked up with Tyrone."

Ray's mouth dropped open in disbelief.

"Yup, he moved in with her—into the house *you* bought. You know he's the one who set you up, right? Yeah, man, he cut a deal with the police, and he got off scot free. Now he got your woman, your house, and your club."

Ray looked at her with fire in his eyes. He was so furious he couldn't speak.

"Just thought you should know, man. I'mma put $100 on your books. Here's my new number if you need to contact me. Let me know if you need anything."

She stood up, kissed him on the cheek, and left. She knew Ray would retaliate. Even locked up he still had juice on the outside. She got Ray out of the picture and would use him to get Tyrone out. With both of them out of the picture, she would have full run of the cocaine distribution in their territory. Yeah, they all thought she was a dumb bitch. She would outsmart them all. She smiled broadly as she got into her new Audi and drove down the highway.

John and Ted prepared for the grand opening of their new business venture. They decided to open a Quiznos together. They went fifty-fifty and were equal partners. Ted put up all the capital but agreed to allow John be an equal partner. It was John's idea, and Ted went along with it. He didn't want to upset John in any way. He knew the man he once loved was capable of anything, and he didn't want to upset him. He didn't want any more trouble, so when John came to him with this business proposition, he agreed. They're goal was to open at least three more stores in the Atlanta area over the next eighteen months. The turnout for the grand opening was great! They made $8,700 in sales!

Kamari and Kennedy worked as cashiers, and Terry and her cousin prepared the sandwiches. John was the manager, and Ted still had his job as captain of the his precinct. They never rekin- dled their love affair but stayed in contact about business matters and never spoke of the Christmas Eve incident again.

Ted buried his guilt by becoming an active member of Anna's church. He was a deacon and a trustee and donated a good por- tion of the money from Donna's life insurance policy to build a youth center for the church. He was determined to turn from his gay lifestyle and believed that God would deliver him from his desire for men.

John began frequenting the local gay bars and had a series of one-night stands before he got smitten by a young man named Artie. Artie was a junior at Union College and majored in business administration. He was very smart and very sexy. John couldn't get enough of him. They had a standing room at the Resident Inn near the airport and spent most of their time there. John thought about just getting an apartment for him but decided to wait and see how business went. He still had two years' free rent, his sever- ance package, stock options, and 401(k) plan from the company. He was pretty well-off financially but was determined not to give Hope one red cent of his money. She was going to pay *him*. The fact that she hadn't even called the girls for weeks played in his favor with the courts. Even though Kennedy would be eighteen in a few months, she would still have to pay for Kamari. He didn't want the money for himself and planned to let Kamari do as she pleased with every dime of it. He just wanted to keep Hope's mind messed up so that she never figured out his lifestyle. That was one of his biggest fears: that Hope would finally realize that all this time John was gay. He was determined to finalize the divorce before she figured it out. He knew that if she actually had a clear mind, sat down, and thought about it, the truth would hit her. Thankfully her mother's death took such a toll on her

that her mind hadn't been right since. Now with the divorce and child support order, she was sure to be almost completely out of her mind. At least that's what John hoped. He wanted to drive her stark raving mad. He made sure the girls never got any of her calls or messages. He wanted them to think that she hadn't even tried to contact them. He wanted them to hate her as much as he did. He couldn't explain his hatred for her, but he hated her guts. He thought that she could change him, but she couldn't, and he resented her for that. His lawyer told him that he'd gotten a response from her attorney contesting the child support and terms of the divorce. Looked like they were in for a long-drawn- out series of hearings before the judge. John was sure the drug dealer's money wasn't as long as his. He would bleed him dry and win. He was in it for the long haul.

It had been six months since Tyrone moved in with Hope. At first, she was a little apprehensive since he was Ray's friend and business partner, but now she was happy she agreed. He took good care of her. He paid all the bills, cooked, cleaned, and kept her cocaine supply stocked. Her habit had gotten quite expensive, and she would never be able to keep it up on her own. She snorted at least a half a gram each day—some days more. Some days she didn't snort at all, but she always made up for it when she started back a day or two later. The drug helped feel alive and kept busy with her online classes that she opted for instead of going into a classroom. This way she could get high. She maintained all A's and was high every step of the way.

Yes, she was starting to feel alive again, but there was a major problem: She felt a void, and she was trying to fill that void with the cocaine. She was estranged from everyone she loved: her chil- dren; her cousin, Patty; her aunt, Ann. And she still missed her mom terribly. She tried not to think about them as much, and the

cocaine helped her do just that. She had become totally depend- ent upon Tyrone for everything. Just the way he had planned.

One night she decided to cook dinner for Tyrone. She thought about extending him a gift that was nice and juicy. It had been six months since it had been touched, and Tyrone had only kissed her on her cheek and forehead. He never made a move or any insinu- ations about sex. He just took care of her. She was beginning to really like him. She looked in the fully stocked freezer and took out two steaks. Later that evening she prepared steak, mashed potatoes, gravy, and string beans. She set the table for two with candles and seductively waited for Tyrone to come home.

By 8:00 p.m. he hadn't come home or called. She repeatedly called his cell, but it went straight to voice mail. It was late, and she was getting hungry. She had used the day to clean up and make dinner so she didn't have anything to eat all day. At ten thirty she tried his cell one last time. When it went to voice mail again, she decided to eat alone. By the time she finished eating she still hadn't heard from him, so she wrapped his plate in alu- minum foil and put it in the oven to keep it warm.

After cleaning the kitchen, she turned on the eleven o'clock news and sat at her computer to work on her paper for her social science class. She poured some coke onto her ever-present mirror and was about to snort her second line when the news reporter caught her attention.

"We're here at Seventh and Arch Streets at a popular nightspot where we've learned that the club's owner has been gunned down…"

"Give me five vials."

Hope reached down into the box and picked up five vials of crack. She opened the slot in the steel door, took the fifty-dollar

bill, and passed the vials to the patron on the other side of the door. She had been working this post for Sheryl for the past year. After Tyrone's death, Sheryl took over the drug operation and had five storefronts with crack booths all around the neighborhood. She was now the biggest crack dealer in the northwest. Hope had nothing else to do and no place else to go so when Sheryl offered to let Hope stay with her; she sold all of her belongings and moved in Sheryl's townhouse. She was able to pay Sheryl rent for about four months before she ran out of money. Sheryl was very understanding, and Hope was grateful. Once again, Sheryl came and offered her a lifestyle that she ran from a long time ago. But *this* was a whole new ballgame.

Crack cocaine had invaded the urban areas of the United States over fifteen years ago and was still wreaking havoc. Crack knew no boundaries. It was now an *epidemic*, meaning it was widespread and had impacted the more affluent members of soci- ety and their families. And Hope was smack-dab in the middle of it. This time it was worse. Crack was a monster. This drug made people do strange and crazy things. It made you forget about eve- rything except your next hit. It destroyed people's lives. Hope sat in the booth from 8:00 p.m. to 8:00 a.m. every day, puffing on her crack pipe and distributing crack to people from all walks of life. Customers ranged from once-prominent businessmen to house- wives. From college students to high school dropouts. She rarely ate and often forgot to shower, brush her teeth, or even comb her hair. All she wanted to do was to smoke and forget about all the pain, hurt, and guilt that were silently killing her. Crack helped her feel dead inside. She cared about no one and felt that no one cared about her. She hadn't seen her children in over a year, and she didn't know what was happening with the divorce proceed- ing, the child support hearings, or the lawsuit that her brother had against her. She had no money. She stayed at Sheryl's house in exchange for working the booth and getting all the crack she could smoke. She had become a walking dead. She didn't care if

she lived or died. Death looked pretty good to her. So much so that she spent the last three days and nights doing nothing except smoking crack. She didn't sleep, she didn't eat, she just smoked crack for seventy-two hours straight.

It was now 8:00 a.m.—time for her to close up shop. She put the bolts on the door and left through the store's front entrance. The manager was coming in to open the store for the day; he was early. She didn't normally run into him.

"Good morning. Rough night, huh? You need to go home and get some rest, honey. You look horrible!"

Hope could tell by the tone of his voice that he was gay. "Thanks," she said as she left. She thought he looked familiar
but couldn't place him and didn't really care.

"Hey, fish!" The manager called after Hope as she walked down the street.

"I know you, don't I? Yeah. I know you. I helped you get your look together. My friend Brenda sent me over to hook you up a few years back. Girl, what happened to you? Oh damn! You found out that your husband was on the down low, didn't you? Girl, don't let that take *you* down! Yours ain't the only husband living a double life! Philly is the down-low capital! Like Atlanta is the gay capital, Philly is the down-low capital."

Hope stared at him blankly. "What did you say?"

"Uh-oh. You didn't know. Come back inside, let me make you a cup of coffee."

He grabbed Hope by the arm and led her frail body back into the store. As he fixed some instant coffee, he told Hope the sor- did story of her husband's double life. Brenda knew; he knew. Hell, everybody knew. Everybody except for Hope!

"The wife is always the last to know, girl."

Hope got up and walked the two blocks to Sheryl's house in a state of shock. All this time she thought that she had done something wrong—that somehow their failed marriage was all her fault. All that time John was gay? She couldn't believe it. Her mind started to travel as she recall all of John's disappearing acts. His lack in interest in making love to her. The many men who always greeted him with compliments on his ties or suits. The long glances he held with strange men when they were together. It all began to make sense to her now, but she still couldn't make any sense of it. It was like she was in a dream. This couldn't be. He couldn't wrap her mind around this. This was more than she could take.

Hope got to Sheryl's house, and it was empty—as usual. Sheryl was rarely there. Once Hope made it clear that she had no desire for a sexual relationship with a woman, Sheryl left her alone. As long as she brought the money from the crack sales in, Sheryl didn't bother her. She went into the bathroom and opened the medicine cabinet where she knew Sheryl kept a stash of oxy- codone to bring her down from her cocaine high. Sheryl didn't smoke crack, but she snorted up a mountain of cocaine daily.

Hope took the bottle and poured out a handful of the pills, went into the kitchen, and filled a tall glass with water, took all the pills two at a time, and lay down on the couch to die. This blow was too much for her to handle. The love of her life was gay. She still felt it was her fault. There was something terribly wrong with her. How could she have fallen in love with a man who was gay? How could she think that he was her prince charming? How could she have loved a man who never truly cared for her at all? Her heart was shattered as she laid her head to rest on the couch.

Soon I will be with my mother again, and everything will be all right, she thought as she drifted off to sleep.

Season of Healing

"Mrs. Daroff, Mrs. Daroff, can you hear me? Can you hear me, Mrs. Daroff?

Open your eyes if you hear me."

Hope could hear someone calling her name, but she didn't want to open her eyes; she wanted to sleep—to die. She won- dered where she was. As the store manager's voice began echoing in her mind she remembered.

You found out that your husband is on the down low, didn't you? A lot of married men are living double lives.

Philly is the down-low capital.

No, no, no. she wanted to die. She couldn't deal with any more grief that this world had to offer.

"Mrs. Darroff. Can you hear me?" the voice said again.

"Leave me alone. leave me alone!" she screamed at the voices telling her to open her eyes. "i just want to die! leave me alone!"

"I'm afraid I can't do that, Mrs. Daroff. As a doctor, I took an oath to save lives; I will do everything in my power to help you live. Can you open your eyes for me, please?"

"no!"

"Okay, Mrs. Daroff. We've pumped most of the pills out of your stomach. How do you feel?"

Hope didn't say anything.

The doctor repeated the question, "How do you feel, Mrs. Daroff?"

Finally, she responded, "I feel like I have to throw up." Then she turned over and threw up on the side of the bed.

"Good! Very good, Mrs. Daroff," the doctor said. "Get it all out of your system." He pushed the Call button for a nurse.

Hope threw up some more, and she continued throwing up until she wretched and had nothing else to bring up. By then the nurse was there and helped her roll over onto a clean bed. Hope turned on her stomach and began sobbing. She heard voices around her but still refused to open her eyes. Soon she fell asleep. She didn't know how much time had passed before she felt some- one nudging her.

"Mrs. Daroff. Wake up, Mrs. Daroff. We need to put an IV into your arm so that you don't become dehydrated. I need you to roll over on your back."

Hope refused to move. "Can't you people just leave me alone? I don't want to live! Can't you understand that?"

"No, Mrs. Daroff. I can't understand why anyone wouldn't want to live. Life is a precious gift. I see so many people every day who have only days left on this earth. I'm sure they would gladly trade places with you in a heartbeat. Now please turn over so I can put this IV into your arm so that you don't dehydrate. We will get you the help you need for you to deal with whatever it is that has you thinking that your life is no longer worth living."

"Can you bring my mother back from the dead? Can you get me my children back from their lying, cheating father who, all the time while we were married, was having sex with other men and making me feel like I was in adequate? Can you get my house back?" She sat up and looked the nurse in the eye. "can you do those things, nurse ratchet?" she screamed.

"Well, I can't bring your mother back, but we can get you a grief counselor. We have people who can help with the situa- tion with your children and get you back in communication with them. There's all types of housing assistance and job placement assistance available. I'm sure you have some very marketable skills. As far as your husband is concerned, well, be grateful that you don't have AIDS. I can take you to a place full of women who've contracted HIV from their partner who, unbeknown to them, was sleeping with other men. You're not the only woman to experience that. But you got away clean—no diseases," the nurse said as she took Hope's arm and inserted the IV. "And my name is Monica, not Nurse Ratchet. This ain't *One Flew Over the Cuckoo's Nest.*"

Hope smiled and kinda chuckled, which made the nurse laugh. "Well, I'm glad I made you smile. Now, you lay here and get
some rest. Would you like something to eat?

"No."

"Well, if you change your mind, just push the button and let me know. Tomorrow a social worker will be in to talk to you, and you'll probably be transferred to another facility."

"What time is it?" Hope asked. "What day is it?"

"Today is Wednesday, September 16, and it's four thirty in the afternoon."

Hope lay in the hospital bed numb. The last date she remem- bered was May 4—the day Tyrone was killed. After that every- thing was a blur. She remembered Sheryl coming to the house that Ray bought; she remembered it went into foreclosure because she was unable to pay the mortgage. Then she remembered Tyrone. Tyrone had been so kind to her and never asked for anything in return. She remembered he was killed and began crying again. She remembered Sheryl giving her a crack cocaine pipe to smoke and after that nothing—except that conversation with the store manager. She still didn't know his name, but she remembered Brenda sent him to spice up her wardrobe. She wondered if Brenda knew John was gay. Of course she did. She remembered that day she saw Brad downtown. He was gay too. She wondered who else was living a double life. As she thought about it she felt nauseous, and she turned to get up and go to the bathroom but couldn't so she threw up on the floor. She hadn't eaten anything, so all that came up was yellow liquid. After throwing up she real- ized that she was hungry and buzzed for the nurse. Monica came in the room.

"You okay, honey? Still sick? At least we know all the pills are out of your system. Don't worry, I'll have someone clean this up right away."

"I'm hungry, Monica," Hope said.

"Good. That's a good sign, Hope. I'll order some chicken broth, crackers, and ginger ale. Let's see how you keep that down."

Hope kept the broth and crackers down and then went back to sleep. A few hours went by; then Hope felt a soft hand rubbing her face and hair.

"Hope! Wake up, cousin. I'm here. I'm going to take care of you." Hope opened her eyes and saw Patty standing over her. She thought she was dreaming, so she grabbed her hand to make sure it was real. Once she realized she wasn't dreaming she opened her eyes, and tears streamed down her cheeks. Patty leaned down and hugged her tightly.

"Oh, cousin! I'm so glad you're all right. I'm so sorry I didn't try harder to reach out to you. I didn't know where you were and had no idea that you were going through all that drama in your life. Sheryl tracked me down and told me she brought you here and that you tried to commit suicide. Don't you know how much you're loved?" She paused as she hugged her tighter.

Oh, so it was Sheryl who bought me here to the hospital. Damn. Sheryl never *comes to the house. Why did she have to come on that par- ticular day? She definitely didn't want no body to be found inside her house. That would lead to an investigation of her and her activities, and she surely didn't want that*, Hope thought as Patty held her.

"Patty, I…I didn't know what to do. Who to turn to. I'm broke. I have no home. My kids don't communicate with me. My mother's son is suing me for selling the house and then…on top of all that…I found out that John is gay and has been throughout our entire marriage," Hope said in between sobs.

Patty sat down on the side of the bed and held her cousin in her arms while stroking her hair. Now she too started crying as she began to feel some of the pain Hope went through.

"I know. Sheryl told me everything. I'm here now. I'll help you sort through all this mess, and you will get over it. You're my cousin, girl! What makes you think that I wouldn't be here for you? You have an eighteen-month-old little cousin whom you've never seen. Guess what her name is? Hope! I named her after you—my sister cousin. I've missed you so much, Hope."

Nurse Monica popped in to see if Hope wanted to try to eat something again. She looked at Patty and recognized her from church.

"You go to Berean, don't you?"

Hope stood up to shake hands with Monica. "Yup, I sure do! You sing on the choir, don't you? How you doin'? I'm Patty, Hope's cousin."

"Nice to meet you, Patty. I'm Monica Hargrove. Glad to see Hope has a visitor. Just wanted to know if she wanted me to order her some dinner."

"I'm *starving*!" Hope chimed in "Yes, please order me some food. Some real food, no broth and crackers. I want some chicken and mashed potatoes and string beans."

Monica laughed. "Okay, Miss Hope. We'll see what we can do." Patty sat in the chair and pulled it closer so she could hold Hope's hand.

"Hope, listen, I know you've been through a lot, but we can get through it together. I want you to come stay with me when you leave here. We have plenty of room in that big ole house. Tomorrow I'll call Maryann and tell her about all your legal needs. Don't worry about money either. I'll handle it."

Hope was so happy to know that she was loved, she began to cry. Patty hugged her tightly until the food came. By the time Hope finished eating, visiting hours were over. Patty promised to come back the next day as Hope fell into a blissful sleep. When she woke the next morning she heard muffled voices in the hall- way. As she sat up, a woman came in and introduced herself as Toni Walker, the social worker.

"Good morning, Mrs. Daroff. We're scheduling you for a transfer to Philadelphia Behavioral Health Center this morning. Since you don't have any health care coverage, I'll need you to fill out these forms so that all of your medical expenses can be cov- ered. Meanwhile, I'll go complete the paperwork for the transfer."

Just then Patty came in. "Good morning, what's going on?" The social worker bought her up to speed about the transfer. "She will need to stay at the center under special care for at least seven days. This is normal procedure when someone tries to commit suicide."

"Oh, okay. Here, Hope, I brought you some clothes, a tooth- brush, hairbrush, and other necessities. Go take a shower and get dressed."

Hope did as she was told. The ambulance arrived an hour later to take her to Belview. She was a little afraid but mostly embarrassed. Now they think she's crazy and are sending her to a place full of real crazy people. She decided to be cooperative so that they wouldn't put any extra labels on her. All the while she blamed John for her being here. She hated him more and more with each breath she breathed. When she arrived, Patty was right there by her side. She arranged for Hope to have a room to her- self and didn't leave until Hope was asleep for the night.

By the fifth day in the facility, Hope was getting up getting dressed and eating with the rest of the group daily. This was one of the things they took into consideration and based her release upon her actions. She was also required to attend three meetings each day before she could be released. She complied with all the rules and by the seventh day was up for release. Patty met with her and the doctors as they reviewed her case before her release.

"We've diagnosed you as bipolar with depression. We're pre- scribing Cymbalta and lithium. You need to take each pill once a day," the doctor said as he gave the prescriptions to Hope.

"Wait a minute," Patty interrupted. "Lithium? She doesn't need that. Cymbalta maybe, but definitely not lithium."

"Oh, it's perfectly okay," the doctor replied. "It's the same medication Martin Lawrence takes."

"She's not taking that. I'll take the prescription for the Cymbalta, and you can complete the paperwork for her release. We're leaving here today with or without your approval. We're out!"

Patty's house was beautiful, and Hope immediately felt right at home. The room they prepared for her was bright with a large window that allowed lots of sunshine in. The walls were a beautiful turquoise color, and the rug was the same color as the walls. The bedspread and curtains were a mixture of turquoise, rose, and white. She even had her own private bathroom. Patty had bought her a few casual outfits, sneakers, pajamas, slippers, underwear, and toiletries. And little Hope. Little Hope was just as cute as she could be. At almost two years of age, she was already potty trained and talked up a storm! She loved singing songs about Jesus and bought Hope fond memories as she sang "Jesus's Love Is A-Bubblin' Over" and "This Little Light of Mine." Hope found herself humming the tunes, as she got ready to join the family for dinner.

Tonight was prayer meeting, and Hope hoped Patty and Bob didn't ask her to go with them. She was hardly feeling God these days. She still felt forsaken by him. He had proven to be like all the other men in her life. He was never there for her and had abandoned her. Just like her father. Just like her husband. Just like Ray and just like Tyrone. In some form or fashion they had all abandoned her. And after all she'd been through, she was sure God didn't want her in his house.

As it turned out, Patty and little Hope stayed home, but Bob went to prayer meeting. He was one of the deacons on duty this week. They were both very active at the Berean Baptist Church. Hope washed the dishes as Patty bathed little Hope and got her ready for bed. As she headed back to her bedroom she heard them singing: "His banner. Over mee. Is love. His banner over me is love. His banner over me is love. His banner over mee is loove."

Hope went to her room. *He does not have a banner over me, and if he does, it certainly isn't love*, she thought as she closed the bed- room door. As soon as she sat on the bed, Patty knocked, cracked the door open, and peeked in.

"Hey, cousin. Can I come in?" "Of course."

She walked over and sat next to Hope.

"Hope. I know you think you don't need counseling, honey, but I disagree. You've been through three *major* life changes. Your marriage is over, your mom died, and you don't have a job. Honey, just *one* of those could take *anybody* off the edge, and here you are going through all of this at the same time! I know we come from a family of strong women, but going to a therapist doesn't mean you're not strong. It means you're smart *and* strong enough to know that you need someone to talk to."

Hope sat in silence, her face like stone showing no emotion. "I made you an appointment with my therapist for tomorrow afternoon at two thirty. She's right downtown. All you have to do is walk to the train station."

"*You* have a therapist?" Hope asked sarcastically.

"Yes, girl, I do. You know what type of lifestyle I was accus- tomed to before I got married. It was a hard adjustment especially after little Hope was born. Girl I thought, I was losing my mind, and so did Bob. He tried everything and told me that if I *didn't* go get some counseling, he would leave. At first I said, 'Good, I want you to go. I don't need you. I can do this on my own.' But deep down inside I knew that wasn't at all what I wanted. I knew I needed to talk to someone. All my pride went straight out the window when I realized that I loved that man and how much he loved me. I now have a family. I would *not* fail as a wife or a mother. Girl, you know how I hate to fail!"

They laughed.

"She helped me tremendously, Hope. That was almost two years ago. I still see her at least once a month, and believe me, it helps. I know it will help you. Promise me you'll go tomorrow."

Hope thought for a moment. She knew she needed to talk to someone.

"Okay. Okay. I promise."

"Good! Now, get yourself a good-night's sleep, and I'll see you in the morning."

After Patty left, Hope sat on her bed for a long time staring into the darkness. Finally she said, "God. I don't know where you are. I don't know if you're real or if all this hype about you is just a lie. I once was a believer—and look at me now. If you *are* real, then you obviously don't care anything about me, but can you please watch over my children?" Then she got under the covers and went to sleep.

"Oooooo, John! I love it!" Artie exclaimed as he ran into John's arms and gave him a long, sensual kiss. He put the one-carat diamond studs in his ears and beamed as he looked in the mirror at the rainbow sparkle reflecting off his ears. "Thank you, baby! Thank you!"

John laughed. He loved to see the joy in Artie's eyes and the happiness in his voice. Artie enjoyed being kept by John, and John liked the idea of keeping him. They were always very dis- creet. Artie was a little feminine, but not overly so as to attract suspicion when they were eating out or shopping. Artie called him Uncle Johnny in public so people assumed they were nephew and uncle. But behind closed doors, Artie called him Big Daddy.

Artie decorated the one-bedroom apartment he leased for him. It was close enough to Union College so Artie could catch the shuttle, but far enough from the other students so that they didn't see John coming and going. Artie didn't have very many friends; he was a bookworm, and half his college tuition was paid from an academic scholarship. His mom was a single parent and spent every dime she had saved to get him down here from Baltimore and pay for books. Grant money paid for the rest of his tuition,

and Artie was also on a work-study schedule—until he met Big Daddy. Now John took care of all his financial needs. As long as he remained discreet, John would continue to take care of him. Artie was discreet, but he was anything but exclusive. He had a few lovers at school but kept that a secret from Big Daddy. He knew John would be furious if he knew anyone else was getting some loving from Artie. He only invited them over during the wee hours of mornings when John was not there. John was easy to read. He was older, and his sexual appetite was not as voracious as Artie's. John enjoyed playing Big Daddy and bestowing gifts. This gave him a sense of control of all things. John was definitely a control freak.

The girls loved their new lifestyle. Kennedy was in her fresh- man year at Harriett Tubman University, and Kamari was on the pep squad. Both girls worked the cash register at Quiznos on the weekends. Kennedy began dating a boy from Union College and wanted to bring him home for Thanksgiving dinner. John was worried because he knew that there were many gay and bisexual boys at Union College. Hell, he was involved with one of them. He was now faced with what he dreaded most: having to school his girls about boys and their sexual tendencies. He did not want them to end up with a man like himself. The thought of that scared him—but not enough to give up his lifestyle. He decided that he would have a talk with both of them—about sex, boys, and the ways of the world. He'd been putting it off but could not continue to do so.

Business was going very well—better than he and Ted had expected. Ted rarely came around; if he wasn't working at the precinct, then he was busy working at church. Driven by the guilt of Donna's death, he rarely slept. He prayed for God to deliver him from homosexuality and believed that God would not only deliver him from homosexuality, but God would also forgive him for the death of his wife. The youth center wasn't complete yet,

but the youth still had needs, and Ted initiated an after-school program and a gymnastics program on the weekends. He made a very conscious effort to stay away from John. He was glad the business was going well. This kept John from bothering

him for money. That's all he wanted anyway. He knew Ted was going to receive a whole lot of money from Donna's life insurance and the home owner's insurance, so when he asked Ted to go half on the Quiznos franchise, Ted felt obligated. He planned to give John
100 percent ownership after the first year so he would be out of his life for good. Ted couldn't believe the way John acted as if that night never happened. There was not a trace of remorse or sorrow in John. All he thought about was money, money, money. It made Ted sick to even think about him. How could he have ever loved a person like that? He had to be careful though. He knew now that John was capable of anything, including murder.

Season of Empowerment

Hope was so excited this morning. She's had five sessions of counseling, and she was feeling good about herself. In just
two months, her life had turned completely around. She signed up with a temp agency after her first session, and they sent her out on assignment two days later. After just thirty days of work- ing as a temp, Turkey Burgers Corporation decided to

hire her as a permanent full-time employee in their real estate department in the headquarters office. She was responsible for making sure that all the stores buildings were kept up to date and up to code. She worked directly with contractors and architects to make sure that the buildings were appealing to the eye, safe, and up to code. They offered her a salary of $65,000 with full benefits, 401(k), and stock options!

Her aunt Ann bought her a 1998 Honda Civic at the auction and paid a whole year insurance policy on it. Aunt Ann, Patty, and Bob had been so good to her. She felt bad about declin- ing their constant invitations to church service and activities. Aunt Ann never really said much—just assured Hope that she was always praying for her. But Hope had no use for God. Of course she would never say that to her aunt, but where had he been all those years that she spent as a faithful servant to and for him? Oh, he must have been busy with someone he deemed more worthy of his blessings. As far as she was concerned, God had left her miserable and in a hopeless marriage to a man who was gay and never loved her. God watched her husband play a game of charades, clothed as a deacon with her and the children being used to complete his masquerade, providing him with the image of a loving husband and a devoted father. God knew all the while that this man was wicked; yet as far as she could see, God chose to bless John and curse her. With all her praying she ended up losing her mother, losing her home, and almost losing her mind. He ended up with a new lucrative business, a beautiful penthouse apartment, a new Mercedes Benz every two years, and he had the children. Nope, she didn't need that kind of God in her life.

Hope's mind-set was that she had alone had the power to change her life. She learned to believe in herself. She learned to love herself. She didn't need God for that; she just needed to look within herself for strength and courage to move on with life and find her new place on this earth. *She* was in control of her own destiny—not God. That's what the New Age movement taught and she believed it. *She* had the power to control her own destiny, and her new employment status proved it. She felt great! She felt empowered! She never started taking the Cymbalta, but she did begin working out every day at the gym at work. She still had her moments of feeling like she was on the verge of a nervous breakdown. Every time she thought about John being gay and her children living with him, she would throw up. But she mastered the art of masking these moments with precision. In hind- sight she could see all the signs. There were times when she was in the middle of a meeting and thoughts would arise. She politely excused herself, went to the ladies' room with one stall, and threw up. Shed splash water on her face, reapply her make-up, and went back to work as if nothing ever happened. No one knew the inner turmoil that she endured daily.

There were some days when she thought she would go stark raving mad, but she kept thinking of how she needed to get her children away from John, and that motivated her and kept her going. Her attorney had appealed the child support decision, and a mediation was scheduled for the divorce proceedings in January. By then, she would have her own place and be pretty well-off but nowhere near living the life she was accustomed to when married to John. Her attorney was sure that she was entitled to spousal support. Yes, she was feeling pretty good today. She was in con- trol of her destiny. "As a woman speaketh, so she is"—this was her mantra, and every day she looked in the mirror and told herself how beautiful she was and how talented she was and that she could do anything she put her mind to. This worked for her. Even though Patty and Bob were happy with her progress, they still thought she needed prayer. She would join them in family prayer, but while they prayed her mind would be a thousand miles away, imagining her new townhouse or condo, a new husband, and the new life that awaited her.

It was the night before the holiday, and Artie didn't go home because he expected to spend the day with John. Unfortunately, John would not be able to spend the holiday with him because he would be spending the day with his daughters. They were cooking dinner together starting tonight, going to the parade in the morning and having dinner that afternoon. Kamari and Kennedy were excited about cooking their first Thanksgiving dinner. Kennedy invited this new boyfriend, and Kamari invited a boy that she had started dating. They were bringing the boys to meet their daddy. That was special, and John wouldn't miss it for anything—not even Artie who was very disappointed. He hadn't seen Artie in about a week because he wasn't feeling well. He'd had a bout of diarrhea, which left him feeling weak. By the time he finished up at the store all he could do was to go home and sleep. He decided to make a surprise visit today since he would be unable to see him tomorrow. He'd make it up to him. He looked forward to making up for lost time.

As he walked toward the apartment he heard music, sounded like Luther Vandross. As he got closer he realized it was defi- nitely Luther.

What is he doing playing Luther? John thought. *He only plays Luther when he's in a seductive mood.* John felt blood rushing to his head as he put the key in the door. He quietly closed the door behind him when he entered. He peeked around the wall from the entrance hallway into the living room where he saw Artie sitting on the couch talking with another young man. They were drinking wine and talking and laughing. Seemed innocent enough, but John decided to watch a while longer to see if any- thing happened.

Artie had been flirting with Todd for months. They had the same trigonometry and biology classes. He knew Todd was dat- ing girls, but there was a twinkle in his eye that told Artie he dabbled with dudes as well. He was one of the few guys who didn't leave campus for the holiday, so Artie invited him over to feel him out. When he accepted the invitation, Artie took it as a sign that he was down. Everybody knows Artie is gay; he made no secret of his sexuality and was not ashamed of it. He knew a lot of guy were secretly sexing other guys but would only been seen with the prettiest girls on campus. These girls were com- monly known as "cover girls"—girls who covered a dude's homo- sexual behaviors—because who would think that a guy with a very pretty girl would want *another guy*?

So, here they were in Artie's apartment, sipping wine and laughing it up. Artie touched Todd's thigh on more than one occasion, and Todd didn't flinch or anything. That was a good sign. Artie picked up the wine bottle to pour some more wine and found the bottle was empty.

"I have another bottle in the fridge. Sit tight. I'll be right back." He turned to go toward the kitchen. John couldn't move fast enough, and Artie saw him and stopped him dead in his tracks.

"Hey...John...I didn't hear you come in."

"I'm sure you didn't," John replied sarcastically.

"Uh...um I thought you weren't coming until after the holi- day was over. Come, meet my friend from school. Todd, this is John. John, this is Todd. John's my roommate."

Todd stood to shake Johns hand; John reluctantly extended his hand.

"Nice to meet you, John." He sensed John was upset. "Artie and I were just sitting here discussing our futures in the world of biochemistry. Since neither of us went home for Thanksgiving we decided to hang out."

"Yes, John," Artie chimed in. "I decided to cook some Cornish hens, stuffing, macaroni and cheese, and some greens for tomor- row so we'll have some food in the house."

"Oh? Are you eating dinner here tomorrow, Todd?"

"No, I'm having dinner with a girl from Spelman at her house with her family. She's bringing me home to meet her dad. I'm a little nervous about that because we're not really a couple; we've just been out a few times. I don't want to send the wrong message, but hey, a Thanksgiving meal is a Thanksgiving meal, right?"

John sat down on the couch. This couldn't be the boy Kennedy was bringing to dinner.

"What's the girl's name?"

"Her name is Kennedy. Kennedy Daroff."

Artie dropped his glass of wine on the floor. John excused himself to the bathroom.

"Uh, listen, Todd. Maybe you'd better leave now. I'll see you in class, okay?"

"*Okay.* I hope I didn't upset your, uh—roommate. I had a nice time tonight."

Artie walked Todd to the door. Before he left, Todd kissed him. John threw up for the third time that day. He had been throwing up daily for the past week or so. He hoped he wasn't coming down with the flu. Once he finished, his mind went back to Todd—and Kennedy. He was already furious about that little nigga being in the apartment drinking wine with Artie. Who knew what would have happened if he hadn't come in? That little nigga had a twinkle in his eye, and he was the boy that his very own daughter was dating. He stormed out of the bathroom with the intention of punching that little nigga in the face and tell him that he is Kennedy's father and that he better not show up for dinner tomorrow. Artie was dabbing the wine out of the carpet, and Todd was nowhere in sight.

"Where's that little nigga at?" he screamed at Artie.

"He left. I told him to leave. I'm so sorry, baby. I had no idea he was dating Kennedy. I knew you were furious, so I made sure he got out of here before you got out the bathroom. Are you okay?"

"Fuck no, I'm not okay, bitch! I came over here to surprise you, and here you are up in the apartment that I pay for, entertaining some nigga—and it turns out to be the boy my daughter calls herself dating!" John turned the coffee table upside down and then threw a lamp at the wall. He stopped and looked at Artie for a few minutes, trying to decide whether or not to kill him, but he couldn't kill him. Todd would certainly testify that John had the opportunity and motive. He thought about just beating the shit out of him but didn't want to bring any attention to their relationship. "You call that nigga and tell him he better not show up at my house tomorrow. And you pack your shit up. I want you out of here by Monday."

John stormed out of the apartment and drove to the closest bar. He needed a drink. He had chills and was sweating at the same time. He needed a few shots of whiskey to clear this cold and his mind.

Hope was really into the Christmas spirit this year! Counseling had really made a huge difference, and she was very happy that she went. A few weeks after Thanksgiving, she found a cute, little three-bedroom house in the Mount Airy section of Philly. She completed the application and paid the $50 processing fee to the realtor and began to envision the house being hers. She meditated on it morning and evening and put a picture of the house on her vision board. The rent was $900 a month, and she needed $2,700 to move in. She only had $700 left in her savings account.

The Honda had conked out and needed a new transmission. Bob got his mechanic friend to take them back to the auction where she ended up getting a 1998 Audi 5000. The mechanic looked it over and said it was in good condition. After paying for the car and paying six months on the insurance premium, she was down to $700 in the bank. But she knew this house was for her and her kids. She just felt it.

A week later, she came home and found a letter addressed to her on her bed. The return address was Dubai. It was a letter from Brenda!

Dear Hope,

I hope this letter finds you in the best of health: mentally, physically and spiritually. I began to get worried about you

when my letters addressed to your old address came back to me marked "Return to sender; addressee unknown." I was worried about quite a few of my friends in the Philadelphia area when I heard about the crack epidemic. André finally wrote me about it a month ago and explained that he had gotten caught up in it but has been clean for eighteen months. He mentioned that he saw you and the shape you were in. He thought that you'd found out about John and that's what drove you to crack. He said the look on your face when he mentioned it let him know that you had no idea. When he learned that you tried to commit suicide that day, he felt terrible. Girl, you sent that boy to church! He said he went to church that Sunday and prayed for forgiveness for opening his big mouth and prayed that you would come through this storm of your life and be a living testimony. Yes, André is serious about his newfound Christianity and loves him some Jesus! He still gay though. LOL.

But back to you, my dear Hope. I'm not a religious woman, but I pray that you have come to grips with this ugly reality. This is one hard and bitter pill for a wife to swallow. Some wives swallow it, accept it, and live with it. That's what I did, for my children's sake. I wanted her to have a two-parent home and as normal a life as possible. Some wives got completely over the deep end never to return. Really, I've seen women go completely crazy to the point they had to be institutionalized. Then there are those who just turn a blind eye. Every clue in the world is right there in front of them, but they refuse to see it. That was you, Hope. I couldn't understand how come you didn't see it. Then I realized you didn't see because you didn't *want* to see. Like I said before, I'm not a religious person, but I believe God didn't allow you to see it at that time because it would have taken you over the deep end. I think he knows what people can handle and at what appointed time. Who knows? You might have killed that nigga! LOL. (I hope you're laughing about this now.)

I heard that you are doing much better but that John is still acting like an asshole and taking you through all kinds of changes. I am so happy that you have weathered the storms of your life, Hope. I want you to call me so we can talk. Call me collect. I've enclosed a check for you to do whatever you need to do—except buy crack! (Smile.)

I love you, Hope. Merry Christmas and I look forward to talking to you soon.

Love, Brenda

Hoped read the letter two more times. She laughed. She cried. Then she looked in the envelope and found a check for $25,000! Hope laughed so hard she began sobbing. This meditating had some bite to it! Not only did she have enough to rent a house, but she also had enough to *buy* a house! But the main reason why she was in such good spirits was because her children were com- ing to spend Christmas with her. Yes, she was definitely feeling the Christmas Spirit—everything seemed to be falling into place. She and Patty were tight again—although they differed in their beliefs. Patty was steadfast in her belief in prayer and God, and Hope was still of the mind-set that she had total control of her own destiny. As long as she thought positive thoughts and kept positive energy around her, things began to turn in her favor.

She didn't pray to God; she meditated. She had a vision board where she pasted pictures of all the things she wanted—her kids, a house, a car, and a husband. She stared at those pictures each morning and each night and meditated on bringing those things into reality. She was glad Patty and Bob continued to pray for her, and not a week went by when they didn't invite her to church. She loved them, but couldn't they see how her life changed for the better since she stopped praying and started taking control of her own destiny? This was working for her. God had never been this good to her. She still felt forsaken by him. If he was real, he

wouldn't have possibly allowed her to go through so much hell on this earth. She didn't ask to be born. She lived according to the commandments of the Bible.

She was an honest, loyal, and faithful wife and mother. And how did God repay her? By sending her a husband who was a complete and total fraud—who never loved her and who was gay. He allowed her home, business, money, and possessions to be taken from her. And then, he let her momma die. He was *not* the God for her. Surely if he had forsaken her, then he definitely had no place for her now. Not after her two affairs. No, she was sure God had forsaken her for good. But she was now in total control of her destiny. The way her life had turned around for the better had proven that to be a fact.

After signing a one-year lease and getting the keys to the house, she made her way around center city doing some Christmas shopping to pass the few hours before it was time to pick her girls up from the airport. Kennedy called the day after Thanksgiving. She was upset and crying about some boy whom she invited over to dinner. She was upset that he didn't show up or called, nor was he answering her phone calls or text messages. She said she'd tried talking to John's girlfriend, Terry, but she needed to talk to her mommy. Hope was able to calm her down and was relieved to learn that Kennedy was still a virgin. She assured Kennedy that the boy was a jerk, and it was better that she learned that now rather than later. They talked for almost an hour; then she talked with Kamari for about forty-five minutes. Kamari told Hope all about her school, boys, and life in Atlanta; and Hope told Kamari all about her new job and the house. Kamari suddenly began cry- ing. She missed her mommy. Then Kennedy started crying again, and Hope started crying too. They spent a good ten minutes just crying on the phone before agreeing that the girls would come spend Christmas in Philly. John didn't object. His whole attitude toward Hope had changed. He had dropped the child support

case and agreed to pay her alimony in the divorce settlement. Hope was tempted to ask him about his lifestyle but decided not to. She remembered how mean and nasty he could be, and since he was being civil right now, she didn't want to rock the boat. She was still very hurt and upset about it but decided now was not the time for that particular battle.

Hope didn't really know their taste anymore, so she decided to let the girls do their own shopping, and she took a stroll down Jewelers Row to pass another hour. She stopped at the window of Banger Jewelers to look at a beautiful multicolored Tahitian pearl strand necklace that was on display. It was gorgeous! She went in to see it up close.

"I haven't seen anything this beautiful in quite some time." She heard a man's voice say. She turned to look, and there stood a tall—about six foot—caramel-brown-colored man with beautiful white teeth, dressed like he came straight out of a *GQ* magazine, smiling at her.

"Yes, it is very beautiful," she said, feeling a bit uncomfortable. "Do you work here?"

"As a matter of fact, I do. Would you like to try it on?" he asked as he went behind the counter and retrieved the keys to open the window display case. He unlocked the display and gently took the necklace out and showed it to her. "Here, feel how soft and smooth each pear is. Here, pull your coat down and let me put it on you."

Hope did as she was instructed, and the gentleman put the necklace on and gave her a mirror. "See the subtle glimmers of blacks and grays giving more dimension to each pearl? This is a very exquisite piece. You have a good eye."

Hope looked in the mirror. It was a beautiful piece of jewelry. "How much is it?" she asked.

"It's on sale: $2,900—originally $3,500."

Hope began to remove the necklace from her neck. "Wow, that's expensive," she said as she gave the necklace back to the salesman.

"Would you like to see something else? Are you looking for anything in particular, or are you just looking?" the man asked as he put the necklace back in the display case.

"Actually I was just looking, passing some time before going to pick my daughters up from the airport. I was thinking of buy- ing myself a piece of jewelry for Christmas, and I wanted some- thing different. That's why that necklace caught my eye."

"Well, why don't you leave me your name and phone number, and I can let you know if the price gets reduced even more after the holidays."

Hope chuckled inwardly at his attempt to get her number. She was going to buy the necklace but decided to play along, so she gave him her business card and told him he could contact her if the price went down. He was very handsome and stirred an interest inside of Hope that she thought was long gone.

"I'm sorry. I didn't introduce myself. My name is Edward Banger. I'd love to show you more of our private collection if you have time."

Hope could have kicked herself. *Edward Banger! He owned the store!*

"Oh, thanks, Mr. Banger, but I don't have time. I need to make my way back to the parking lot, get my car, and drive to the air- port. Maybe some other time."

"I look forward to it, Ms. Daroff. Wait. Let me give you my card." He went to the counter and wrote something on a business card. "This is my work number, this is my cell number, and this is my home number. You can reach me any time. I look forward to

hearing from you." He gave her the card, helped her put her coat on, and walked her to the door.

"I hope to talk to you again before the holidays, but if I don't, you have a very merry Christmas, Ms. Daroff."

"You too, Mr. Banger. And thanks!"

Hope rushed down the street as snowflake began to fall. The temperature had dropped that fast, but she felt warm and fuzzy inside. It was certainly beginning to look a lot like Christmas! *Ed Banger was phine!* Hope hadn't had an interest in any man since Tyrone. She had no interest in developing feelings for a man again only to then be abandoned by him. Nope. She was just so focused on getting her life back in order, and a relationship of any kind wasn't even on her radar. She got in her car and drove to the airport thinking that Mr. Banger was so fine that he *had* to be gay. Her gaydar was in high gear, and everyone was suspect until proven otherwise. She shook off Mr. Banger as she walked to gate 5 to meet her girls.

It was Christmas Eve, but it didn't feel like it. John was used to cold weather and snow around Christmastime. Here in Atlanta it was 75 degrees. The streets were crowded with people wearing short sleeves and sandals instead of fur coats, hats, and gloves. He was beginning to get homesick. He missed the girls. Terry was spending the holidays with her boyfriend, and John suspected that she would move out soon. She had been seeing this guy for about five months, and as far as dude knew, John was her uncle, and Kennedy and Kamari were her little cousins. She had been a great help with the girls and kept his secret life a secret from them. He gave her $5,000 before she left. She was surprised and promised to come back when the girls returned. John decided

that he would call her tomorrow, wish her a merry Christmas, and tell her to go on and live her life and be happy.

John made his way through the crowds downtown, taking his time getting to his destination: his doctor's office. He called John this morning and asked him to come in. John suspected that he might be HIV positive. He had all the symptoms. He just needed to get on that medication. He wasn't too worried; he knew plenty of guys who were living fine with HIV—as long as they took their meds.

"Mr. Daroff, I'm glad you could make it in on such short notice." Dr. Goldstein shook John's hand as he motioned for him to sit down.

"I don't know how to tell you this, but to just come out and say it. Your tests came back positive for the AIDS virus. You have full-blown, AIDS Mr. Daroff."

John was shocked. Full-blown AIDS? Not just HIV positive but full-blown AIDS? His eyes welled up with tears. "How much longer before I die?" he asked.

"Well, we can give you some meds to help with the symptoms. If you had gotten tested earlier before it got to be full blown, you could have survived. I could be more hopeful about your longevity. But with full-blown AIDS…well…six…maybe eight months."

John quietly got up and left. He calmly walked down the hall- way, got on the elevator, and walked to his car. He got in, opened the glove compartment, pulled out a .38, put it in his mouth, and pulled the trigger.

Season of Restoration

Hope always hated shopping on Christmas Eve, and this year was no different. She never understood why people waited until the last minute to do their Christmas shopping. This was a tradition that John had with the girls, and since they were with her this year, she felt obligated to carry on the tradition that they were used to. Kamari was so easy going and easy to please. She only wanted to shop at the Gap and Aeropostale. Hope made her get two dressy outfits from Bloomingdales. She was sixteen now and needed to learn to dress for different occasions. Yes, Kamari was a delight. Kennedy, on the other hand, had become bitter and nasty toward Hope. She disagreed with everything Hope said and gave her word for word about every little thing. It was like she thought she was the mother. Hope was trying very hard to be patient. She understood that Kennedy could be harboring some ill feelings toward her and that she had been playing the role of mother for the past two years. She was very protective over Kamari—understandably so—but Kamari seemed to be getting irritated too. Kamari was happy that she was with her mommy and did not want Kennedy bossing her around.

When Hope picked out the two dressy outfits, Kennedy turned her nose up and said, "Oh no, those outfits look too old for her. Come on, Kamari, we'll go look in Macy's."

While Hope was counting to ten before responding, Kamari told her, "I like both the outfits my mommy picked out for me. You need to mind your damn business."

Kennedy looked surprised and hurt but didn't say another word about it. When they'd finished shopping, Hope suggested that they go to Bookbinders for dinner. Kennedy turned her nose up and said she would prefer Le Bec-Fin.

Kamari came to the rescue again. "Nobody wants Le Bec- Fin. They give you a small piece of steak and three green beans and charge $100. I want seafood. Let's go to Bookbinders like Mommy said."

Hope chuckled to herself as she wrapped her arm around Kamari and began walking down Market Street with Kennedy dragging her feet behind them.

Hope could have never imagined that her relationship with her firstborn would be this strained. She remembered when she first found out that she was pregnant with Kennedy. Her mother had just been diagnosed with breast cancer and had seemed to give up on life until she learned that she was going to be a grand- mom. It was like she found something to live for, and she fought that cancer and won. Kennedy was her mother's pride and joy. She realized too that Kennedy was still mourning the loss of her grandmother. Hope suggested that they seek counseling.

"We had counseling sessions with my dad, and we're all fine. Maybe it's *you* who needs the counseling."

It took everything Hope had to keep from choking her to death. Kennedy had always been a Daddy's girl, and no matter what, he could do no wrong as far as she was concerned. Hope didn't understand it. She realized it was her fault because she

always covered for John and made him look like a king in their daughter's eyes. While Hope struggled to make sure they had everything they asked for under the Christmas tree each year, she always gave John the credit. She told them about how hard their dad worked to keep a roof over their head and to keep the lights on, etc., etc., but all the time it was her who sacrificed to pay all the bills. Now, as far as

Kennedy was concerned, her daddy was the king and had done everything to keep the family together, and Hope was the witch, the villain who destroyed everything her daddy worked so hard for. Hope's heart was heavy, but she didn't see the point in telling Kennedy the truth now. She would probably think Hope was lying anyway, and it would make things worse, so she just sucked it up and hoped for the best.

After dinner, they dropped the bags off at home and hurried off to meet Patty, Bob, and little Hope at church. Little Hope had a small part in the Christmas play, and Kennedy and Kamari didn't want to miss it. They loved that little girl, especially Kennedy. Her whole countenance lit up when little Hope was around.

This church was *always* crowded. This was one of the reasons Hope never wanted to come. First, they drove around trying to find a parking spot. They finally found a spot five blocks away from the church. It took them fifteen minutes to walk to the church, but they finally got there and on time. The play hadn't started yet, and Patty was in the lobby area talking to a very handsome gentleman. He looked familiar, and as she got closer she realized that Patty was talking to Mr. Banger!

"Hey, Hope!" Patty said as she grabbed the three of them in a group hug.

"You all are just in time. Bob is holding our seats up front." "Hello, Ms. Daroff.

Wow, this is a pleasant surprise. What a
small world!"

Hope smiled as she replied, "Yes, it is. Good to see you again, Mr. Banger."

"Please, call me Ed. Can I call you, Hope?"

Hope was distracted as she saw Kennedy bend over to whisper something in Kamari's ear. Apparently Kamari didn't like what she said because she punched Kennedy in the arm.

"Yes, you can call me Hope. These two young ladies are my daughters, Kennedy and Kamari. Girls, this is Mr. Banger. We met at his jewelry store the day I picked you up from the airport."

Kamari extended her hand for Ed to shake. "Nice to meet you, Mr. Banger."

Kennedy just waved and said, "Aunt Patty can we go in now? I don't want to miss anything."

"Yes, let's go in. It was good seeing you, Ed. Come on, ladies, let's go to our seats. Hope, we're sitting in the center right aisle on the fourth row." Then she rushed off with the girls, leaving Hope standing there with Ed Banger.

"Well, I'd better get inside to my seat too. My granddaughter is making her debut in tonight's pageant. My son and his wife are waiting for me upstairs. What are you doing after the service?"

"We still haven't decorated our tree. We always do it on Christmas Eve. This is the first Christmas I've spent with my girls in two years, so we'll just spend a quiet night at home, deco- rating, baking cookies, and wrapping gifts."

"Oh. I see. That sounds nice. I'll probably go to my son's house and spend the evening with them. Are you a member here?"

"No. I'm just visiting. This is my first time here actually. This church is huge. Too big for me."

"Yes, it is big, but there are several ministries and always some- thing to do to help spread the gospel and have good clean fun.

Most importantly, the Word of God is taught, and souls are being fed. I hope you don't let the size discourage you from joining. I think you'll like it."

Hope laughed. "Well, I don't have to ask if you're a member." Ed laughed too.

"I've been a deacon here for four years. I joined about six years ago. I had never been a churchgoing man, but after my wife passed away, I went on a binge. I was an alcoholic. My oldest son has been a member here for about ten years, and he got me to come with him one Sunday. I was still an alcoholic, but I started coming every Sunday. One day I found myself up at the altar—joining. They asked me questions about myself, and I shared that I had a problem with alcohol. One of the ministers contacted me and went with me to my first AA meeting. That was November 28, 1988. I haven't had a drink since that day."

"Wow. That's a beautiful thing," Hope replied. She was begin- ning to get nervous for some reason. "Well, let me make my way inside. It was really good seeing you, Mr.…uh. I mean Ed. Merry Christmas."

"Merry Christmas to you too, Hope. Do you still have my numbers?"

"Yes. Yes, I do."

"Well, give me a call over the holidays. I only have your work number. You didn't give me your home number."

Hope pulled out a piece of paper and a pen to write down her home number. Her hands were shaking as she gave it to him.

"Here you go, Ed. Call me when you get a chance."

"Thanks. How 'bout tomorrow evening…after all the holi- day festivities die down. Maybe we can talk or go out for coffee or something."

"Maybe. I'll talk to you tomorrow," Hope replied as she hur- ried off into the sanctuary.

Kamari had saved her a seat next to her. "Sit here, Mommy. It's just about to begin."

The choir was singing one of her favorite Christmas songs, "O Holy Night." It was a very large choir, and they sounded good. Next the pastor came out and gave his welcome, greetings, and prayer. He seemed genuine, and the congregation was very recep- tive to their pastor. Then there was a drum presentation, and a group called Steppers for Christ performed. They were right up Kamari's alley! She enjoyed them so much she told Hope that she was joining this church. Hope just smiled outwardly and hugged her baby girl. But her insides were trembling. She still had beef with churches and with God himself. She was not ready to join any church, but she would support her daughter in any way. She was still hoping that they would stay with her permanently. It was evident that Kamari wanted to, but Kennedy had her heart set on returning to Atlanta in January. She didn't want her daughters to be separated, but things seemed to be heading in that direction.

After the play, they greeted all the players and took lots of pictures with little Hope. She was so adorable and excited about Christmas. She wanted Kennedy and Kamari to spend the night with her, but Kennedy told her they wanted to be home when Santa came to their house, but they would come over in the morning. She was a totally different person with little Hope, and as soon as they left her presence, the smirky scowl returned to her face. As they walked back to the car all Kamari could talk about was the Steppers for Christ and the cute boys on the drums.

"They are much cuter than the boys in Atlanta. I can't wait to join the Steppers. I wonder if you have to try out."

Once they got home, Kennedy and Kamari decorated the tree, while Hope wrapped presents. They sang along to the Motown Christmas music and baked cookies. At midnight Kamari was about to burst, so Hope gave them their presents. Kamari opened her box that contained an eighteen-carat, eighteen-inch gold chain with her name and a diamond over the letter I. She was ecstatic as she jumped up and down, grabbed Hope, and gave her a big hug and kiss.

Kennedy opened her box, which contained a sixteen-inch strand of cultured pearls and a pair of pearl earrings with dia- mond baguettes surrounding the pearl. She balled the necklace up, threw it back in the box, then looked at Hope, and said, "Thanks." Hope's heart dropped.

"You're welcome, baby," she said. "Well, I'm exhausted. I'm going to bed. See you ladies in the morning."

Kennedy didn't say a word, just sat there with that smug look on her face. Kamari noticed too and tried to make up for her sister's lack of gratefulness and enthusiasm.

"Good night, Mommy. Merry Christmas! And thank you for the necklace! I love it!"

"And you too! I'm going to bed too. Good night, Kennedy." Hope had just climbed into bed when the phone rang. She knew it was Patty before she answered.

"Hello, Patty."

Patty laughed. "Girl, you knew I had to call you. How do you know, Mr. Handsome, Ed Banger? I've been trying to get you to church to introduce you to him, and here you already met him— and you didn't even tell me!"

Hope laughed, and told Patty about her first encounter with Ed Banger.

"He's a nice man, Hope. His wife died from an asthma attack about six years ago. He's dated about a handful of women that I know of, but nothing serious. He seems to like you too. Do you like him?

"I don't know the man enough to say whether I like him or not. Don't go playing matchmaker, cousin, you hear?"

Patty laughed. "Okay, but he is the catch of the day! Merry Christmas and I will see you guys tomorrow. I'll probably be up all night preparing for the brunch here tomorrow. I pretty much have everything done though. Will you help me serve?"

"Of course, I will. Good night. And merry Christmas, cousin. I love you."

Hope climbed under the covers when the phone rang again. *Patty must have forgotten something*, she thought.

"Hello?"

"Hello, Hope. This is Ed. Ed Banger, I'm sorry to call you so late, but I wanted to ask you if…uh…um…well…if I could sit with you during service tomorrow."

Hope removed the receiver from her ear and looked at the phone. Then she looked at the clock. It was 1:30 a.m. Was he serious?

"Well, I guess so…if we see each other. You know how crowded your church is."

"I'll have the ushers save us seats, and I will wait in the lobby area until I see you. Since you are a visitor, I want to make sure you have a good experience, and that starts with a good seat. Again, I'm sorry for calling so late, but I sat here for two hours contemplating whether or not to call you, and I finally got up the nerve to do so."

Hope was silent; she didn't know what to say. Finally she said just the right thing.

"Well, I'm glad you called, Ed. I look forward to seeing you tomorrow."

She could hear the smile on his face as he said, "Me too, Hope. Good night."

Kamari couldn't sleep. Kennedy was getting on her last nerve, and she was going to tell her about it herself. Kennedy was so startled when she stormed into her room that she jumped up out of the bed.

"What is wrong with you, Kennedy? Ever since we got here you've been just mean and evil toward Mommy, and I want to know why."

"Because she's a stupid whore. She's had how many boyfriends since she and Daddy divorced? Three? Four? And she's working on number 5. Daddy has only had one woman since Mommy. She deserted us. I've been more of a mother to you than she has. She was on drugs, lost all her money and her house. Now she's trying to act like she has it all together. Where was she when we needed her? Where was she when you graduated from eighth grade? When you started high school? Daddy was the one who was there for us, not her. Now she thinks because she wanted us to come here for Christmas that makes up for everything? Well, it doesn't, Kamari. Don't forget that *she* deserted us, and *Daddy* was the one who was there for us and took care of us."

"i don't care, kennedy!" Kamari screamed. "Mommy has always taken good care of me. She just took it real hard when G'mom died, and she went through some changes. She didn't desert us. *You* wanted to go to Atlanta, and I followed *you*. *You* wanted to stay, so I stayed. I think that when we chose not to come back that hurt Mommy even more. Maybe she did do some things wrong, but she's getting herself together, and I'm proud of her. I love Mommy no matter what. I love Daddy too, but I love Mommy too. I can love them both equally, but you can't. You are not my mother. You can't take her place, Kennedy. Your heart is hardened, and I really don't understand why. But you need to get your act together and give my mother the respect she deserves.

You may not love her, but you need to respect her simply because she's your mother. Now, good night!"

Kennedy couldn't believe the way Kamari had just spoken to her.

Your heart is hardened, and I really don't understand why. But you need to get your act together and give my mother the respect she deserves.

Kamari's words resounded in her mind over and over again.

My heart is hardened because she deserted us. She just left to go do what she wanted to do. Drugs and men. She didn't care about us. Only Daddy cared. He did everything for us. She barely even called us—not even on our birthdays or holidays. She gets no respect from me, and I can't wait to go home, Kennedy thought as she cried herself to sleep.

When they arrived at church Christmas morning, Ed was waiting for them in the lobby just like he promised. His face lit up when he saw Hope.

"Merry Christmas!" he exclaimed as he hugged her. He said Merry

Christmas to Kennedy and Kamari and he hugged them too.

Kamari giggled and said, "Same to you." Kennedy said,

"Thanks."

The service was awesome. The Praise Dancing group per- formed, the choir sang a medley of Christmas hymns, and the preacher *preached*! He preached from an entirely different perspective—he spoke about Joseph.

"Some of you women complain about there not being any good men, but the truth is there are plenty of good men out here. When you see one, you just don't recognize him, but that's another sermon for another day. Today I'm gonna tell ya'll about a *good* man. People don't often talk about Joseph. Joseph doesn't

get his props. Can you imagine being engaged to a virgin, and she shows up and tells you she's pregnant, but she's still a virgin! Most men would be like, 'Yeah right! I'm out.' But Joseph didn't say that. Even before the angel appeared to him and told him that what Mary said was true, he was still faithful and planned to divorce her quietly so he wouldn't disgrace her. Joseph raised Jesus as his own. He didn't even touch Mary until after Jesus was born. Now. *That's a good man*!

Ed was on his feet during the sermon, clapping and scream- ing, "Amen! Preach, Pastor!"

Hope enjoyed the service. As they walked toward the lobby, she found herself inviting Ed to brunch at Patty's. Of course he accepted; he would come after he left his son's house. His family didn't make it to church, and he promised his granddaughter that he would come by to see what Santa bought her.

Hope didn't see Patty, and it was so crowded, she decided to just go on over to the house. As they walked to the car, Kamari went on and on about the Steppers team.

"I can't wait to join both those group, Mommy! Did you see they had *all* ages on the dance group? I wonder if you have to audition to join."

She went on and on until Kennedy rudely interrupted. "That's a heathen church. My dad's church would not have any drum- mers and steppers in the sanctuary. That was a disgrace. I'm not joining that church. I'm going back to my dad's church."

"Well, you go right ahead with your stuck-up self. I'm join- ing Berean. Everybody doesn't praise God the same way. I felt the Holy Spirit in that churches—even the people are friendly. I'd heard about this church before we went to Atlanta and have wanted to visit here. Daddy's church is dry and dull, and they don't do anything for young people. Kennedy, you never have anything nice to say. You've been acting nasty since we got to Philly. I can't wait until you go back to Atlanta."

"You mean until *we* go back, don't you?" Kennedy asked as they approached the car.

"No. I mean *you*. I'm not going back. I'm staying here with Mommy. I'm joining this church, and I'm going to enroll in Central High School."

Kennedy was about to open the passenger door that was on the street side. She turned around to walk back toward Kamari when a car suddenly came speeding toward them. Before they knew it, Kennedy had been struck.

"Oh God. Oh God! no! Please, God, please! Not my baby! Help! Somebody, help!" Hope and Kamari were both crying and screaming for help. There were so many people around they could hardly breathe.

"Back up, give them some room. somebody call an ambu- lance. quick." She heard a familiar voice. She looked up, and it was Ed.

"It's okay, Hope. I'm so sorry. Listen, everything is going to be fine." He bent over to check Kennedy's pulse. "Her pulse is good, and she's breathing." He turned toward the crowd.

"Can you please back up? She needs air. She's breathing and has a good pulse. I think she'd going to be just fine."

Hope was in shock. She felt like she was in a dream. Everything seemed muffled, and she could barely make out what Ed was say- ing. She had Kennedy's head in her leg and was stroking her hair, while Kamari held her hand and rubbed her arm. Then the paramedic arrived. They told Hope to let them take Kennedy, but Hope didn't move. She felt Ed take her by the arms and lift her up. Kamari came over to help him. Everything was a fog. She saw them put Kennedy into the ambulance and heard the paramedics

mumbled something to Ed, and he mumbled something back. Then Ed took her car keys, put her and Kamari in the car, and he drove them to the hospital. She could hear Kamari crying, but she couldn't move or talk.

Please, God. Please let this all be a bad dream," she thought as she closed her eyes. She felt the car come to a stop and opened her eyes. She watched Ed and Kamari get out of the car. Ed came around, opened her door, and helped her out of the car. And he and Kamari helped her walk into the hospital. She saw a sign that said Emergency, but she couldn't hear anything—not even mumbling. She saw a doctor coming toward them, and he was saying something to her, but she couldn't hear him. He just stared at her blankly because she couldn't talk either. The doctor said something to Ed, and then he started talking to Kamari. She watched Kamari walk over to the nurse's station where they gave her a phone. A nurse came over and gave Hope a pill and a cup of water. Hope took it, and Ed sat her down on the couch. She saw Patty coming toward her with tears in her eyes. She grabbed Hope and hugged her. She could see Ed's lips moving as he was talking to Patty, and she saw Patty lift her hands up to the sky and started clapping. Hope laid her head on Patty's lap and went to sleep.

Harold heard the phone ringing, but he couldn't get up to answer it. His mind was aware that he needed to answer the phone, but his body wasn't cooperating and his head was pounding. Finally the phone stopped ringing.

What day is it? he thought. Then he remembered: It was Christmas Day. Yesterday was Christmas Eve, and he found out that he had AIDS. He tried to kill himself, but when he pulled the trigger of the gun he kept in his glove compartment, there were no bullets in it. He was sure Terry emptied them out. She was always on him about having a loaded gun around. When that didn't work, he went to the nearest bar and drank until they wouldn't serve him any more. Somehow he was able to drive himself home, and he and Jack Daniels spent the rest of the evening together.

Ring. The phone started ringing again. John opened his eyes and stared up at the ceiling.

Ring.

He realized he was on the couch and finally sat up and saw that the phone was right there on the coffee table.

"Hello?"

"Daddy?" Daddy! You have to come to Philly. Kennedy has been in a terrible accident. She was hit by a car, and the doc- tors say they don't know if she'll ever walk again, and she's still unconscious."

John shook his head a few times trying to understand what he just heard.

"What!?"

"Daddy, we need you to come to the hospital as soon as pos- sible. Mommy is incoherent. She can't handle it, and they need someone to make decisions."

John took a long gulp of the Jack Daniels that was in the glass on the coffee table.

"What hospital?" he asked as he refilled the glass. "Yorkhood."

"Okay. I'll be there as soon as I can, pumpkin."

John gulped down two more shots before he got up and called the airline to book a flight into Philadelphia. This was the last place he expected to be going back to—ever. He thought he had left Philly in his past. But he had to get to his daughter.

He booked a flight that would leave in two hours. He called a cab, took a quick shower, threw some things into a suitcase, and headed out the door.

John tried to sleep during the three-hour plane ride, but even after three more shots of Jack Daniels, he was wide awake. He was worried about his baby. He wanted to pray, but it had been so long, and he had done so many ungodly things that he didn't think it would be any use. But still, he put his head in his hands, bent forward, and said, "Lord, please heal my baby girl. Take me instead. Amen."

He sat back in his seat and began thinking about his life. He thought about his childhood, his first lover, but most of all he thought about what a horrible husband he had been to Hope. He began to feel remorseful about all the things he had done to her. He finally admitted to himself that he was a gay man. He was jealous of Hope. He always hated the way men looked at her. He wanted them to look at him that way. He wanted the attention from men that she always got. He began to compete with her in everything, and before he knew it, he had built up a hatred for Hope. He hated her for being everything he wanted to be. For being a woman. The more she tried to love him, the more he hated her. He made her think it was her fault, but it wasn't. It was his own fault. He realized that he didn't hate her; he hated himself. He hated that he had to pretend to be something that he wasn't. It wasn't Hope's fault that he was gay. She didn't even have a clue. All of a sudden he felt sick. He ran to the bathroom and vomited until he wretched and there was nothing else to bring up. He washed his face, looked at himself. He took a long, hard look at himself and began to cry uncontrollably. How and when did he become such a monster?

Oh God! Oh God! Please don't punish me by taking my daughter. God, I confess my sins. I'm a murderer, a liar, a thief—just a wretched,

wicked soul. I repent from my wicked ways, God. Please forgive me, Lord. Please forgive me. Please, Lord, forgive me and save my baby."

The rest of the trip seemed to go by ever so slowly. He thought about his life and how it had gotten to this point. He thought about his first encounter with Rickey. Rickey was a boy from church. He was light skinned with green eyes. The exact oppo- site of John. They sang on the choir together, they were in the Boy Scouts together, and they often spent the night together. He remembered the first time Rickey French-kissed him and sucked his genitals. He fell in love with Rickey that night. John tried to tell his mother about his feelings, but she refused to hear it.

"Ain't no son of mine no faggot. Don't bring no shame on me, boy. You better start spending more time with some of those little girls and less time with pretty Rickey."

It was the same when he tried to tell her about the deacon and choir director at church. She quickly changed the subject and let him know that she did not want to hear what he was trying to tell her. "Those are good men. They take time out to spend with you and teach you how to be a man. More than your daddy ever did. You better appreciate them and listen to them and do whatever they tell you to do."

It wasn't until her funeral that he learned that these men gave his mother a monthly allowance to help with her expenses.

Years went by, and he and Rickey continued their love affair in secret. Rickey was a star basketball player and was on his way to play professional ball in Spain. The night before he left, John's mother caught him and Rickey kissing, and she beat the shit out of John with a frying pan and threw him out of the house. He was nineteen years old. His lover was off to another country, and he was out on his own home. He did what he had to do in order to survive the streets of Philly. He hooked up with an older guy named Harold who took him under his wing. Harold had a wife

and kids but had a thing for young boys. At first John stayed at the house with the family, but soon John helped him get an apart- ment so they didn't risk getting caught. Harold also owned an electrical contracting company and taught John all about being an electrician. He gave him an apprenticeship and trained him to journeyman and foreman. By the time he was twenty-two, John was making $40 per hour. Then Harold introduced him to the business that helped finance the electrical contracting company: cocaine. Harold was also one of the main cocaine suppliers in the city. Once he bought John into that end of the business, things began to go downhill. The cops raided his place, but Harold had taken a trip back to the Dominican Republic, and John was in his apartment and the cops hadn't been trailing John. Harold never came back, so a few of his runners got sent up for a bid, and John never saw or heard from Harold again.

John joined the electricians' union and was able to work pretty steadily. He wanted his mom to be proud of him, so he started dating girls. When he met Hope, he knew she was just the right girl to take home to his mother. He recalled the first time he saw her. She was having lunch at an outdoor café downtown. He was on lunch too and was dressed in his work clothes: Carharts and Timberlands. It was April, and the weather had just broken. She was wearing a yellow dress, black jacket, and black pumps. Her legs were long and beautiful. Her hair was long and full, and her skin was clear caramel brown. He stood watching her while he waited for his order, and when she laughed showing deep dim- ples and pretty white teeth, he was smitten. He asked the waitress if she came there often and was told she came about every other day. He told her to ring up their order, and he paid the tab. He watched each day to see if she went there, and sure enough after that Monday, she came Wednesday and Friday with the same girlfriend. He paid the tab again on Wednesday, and this time she stopped him as he was leaving.

"Hey, thanks for paying for our lunch again today. You should have come and sit with us."

John was shy and kind of embarrassed about his appearance. "You're welcome. I didn't want to come over dressed like this though."

"Well, maybe I can see you in your regular clothes sometime. Here's my number. You can give me a call if you'd like."

John smiled and took her number. On their first date he took her to see Luther Vandross and then to 2020 Restaurant. She was fun, smart, and pretty. He liked her and began dating her on a regular basis. After about six months, Hope got pregnant. John took her to meet his mother and told his mom that he was thinking about marrying her. He didn't tell her that she was preg- nant though.

He didn't know his mom had been diagnosed with cancer. She kept that from him. But she let him know that she was proud of the man he had become and that she wanted lots of grandbabies. John promised to be a good husband and father and promised her lots of grandchildren. She died shortly before Kennedy was born. John felt like it was his duty to marry Hope and become a fam- ily man. He wanted to keep his promise to his mother. She had raised him all by herself, and he never knew his father. He would never allow his children to feel the hurt of not knowing their dad.

"Ladies and gentlemen, please put your seatbelts on as we pre- pare to land at the Philadelphia International Airport."

John rushed through the airport. He only had a carry-on so he didn't have to wait for his luggage. Once outside, he flagged down a cab and jumped in.

"Abington Memorial Hospital."

Season of Deliverance

Hope opened her eyes. At first she didn't know where she was. The room was unfamiliar. Then she remembered: Kennedy had been hit by a car, and she was in the hospital. She sat up and realized she was in some type of waiting room, but there was no one else there. She didn't know what time it was, but it was dark outside. She wondered if it was still Christmas. She tried to stand but felt dizzy, so she sat back down. Patty peeked in the room.

"Hey, cousin. How are you feeling?"

"I'm okay…a little dizzy. What's happening? What's going on with Kennedy?"

"The doctors say she is going to be okay. John is—" "John? John's here?"

"Yes. Kamari called him when you passed out. The doctors needed consent to perform the operation."

"What operation? Why did she need an operation, Patty?" "Well. Hope, the doctor said—"

"Hey! How are you feeling? You want some tea? Coffee? Water? Anything?" Ed said as he entered the room.

"No. No thank you. What operation, Patty?"

"They had to do a spinal operation, Hope. It went well, but they can't tell if the paralysis is temporary or not yet."

"Paralysis!"

"Yes, she can't feel anything or move anything from the waist down. She has a catheter, but she woke up and talked to us for a while. She's sleeping now."

"Where's Kamari?"

"She went with John to help him check into his hotel. He doesn't look well."

Who cares? Hope thought. "Take me to see

Kennedy."

Ed came over to help her up. "What time is it?" she asked him

"It's five thirty," Ed answered. "am or pm?"

"pm."

"Wow, you mean I've only been sleep for a few hours? It seems like I was out for a long time."

"Hope, it's 5:30 p.m. the next day—the day after Christmas. You were sleep for a long time, Hope."

He walked her to Kennedy's room in the ICU. The doctor came in and explained the situation to her.

"Mrs. Darroff, I'm glad to see you up and about. Your husband consented for us to perform a surgical procedure on Kennedy's spine. We were able to stop the swelling; now we have to wait and see."

Hope took Kennedy's hand, and the memories began to flood her mind. Memories of her birth, her first birthday, her first steps, her first potty, her first day of kindergarten. How did

they get here? Why was she so angry with me? She learned over and kissed Kennedy on the forehead. Kennedy opened her eyes, looked at Hope, and smiled.

"Hi, Mommy," she managed to say.

"Did you see Daddy? Daddy's here. Everything is going to be okay."

Tears streamed down Hope's cheeks.

"Yes, baby. Everything is going to be fine. You get some rest now. Mommy will be right here."

Kennedy smiled, closed her eyes, and went back to sleep.

"I can take you home to shower if you want to," Ed said as he passed her a cup of coffee.

"No, no. I'm gonna stay here."

"Mrs. Darroff, she'll probably be asleep for the rest of the night. It would be fine if you went home and came back in the morning. We won't know anything different until then."

"Yes, Hope. Come, honey, let's get you home where you can take a nice, hot bath and eat something. You haven't eaten in two days! I still have a whole Christmas dinner for you—turkey, stuffing macaroni and cheese, kale, candied yams, mashed pota- toes, string beans, peach cobbler, apple pie," Patty rambled off the dinner menu.

Hope felt her stomach rumble at the thought of food. She looked at her daughter sleeping so peacefully and decided it might be a good idea for her to go home and freshen up. She probably looked a hot mess. She didn't want Kennedy to wake up and see her this way. Yes, it had been two days. Yesterday was Thursday— Christmas Day—one Christmas she would never forget. And she hadn't eaten yesterday or today. She was famished.

"Okay. Okay." She smiled. "You've convinced me."

Ed helped her on with her coat and walked them to Patty's car.

"I'll ride with Patty, Ed. Thanks for everything."

"No problem. I'm glad I was here. I'll call you later." He opened the passenger side door, bent over, and kissed her on the cheek.

As soon as Patty got in, Hope started. "So, that punk-ass fag- got John is here, huh?"

"Now, Hope, don't be like that. He looks like he's been to hell and back."

"What! I'm the one who has been to hell and back. He punk ass couldn't have survived what I have been through. Whatever he's been through is nothing but karma. All the shit that punk- ass bitch has put me through? Ha! But still I rise!"

"Only by the grace of God, Hope. Only by the grace of God," Patty replied.

Hope sucked her teeth and rolled her eyes, but didn't utter another word. Silently she thought that it may have been the grace of God that kept Kennedy from being killed, but she didn't say so out loud.

John woke up to a sick feeling in his stomach. He ran to the bathroom and began throwing up. This was becoming routine. It had been three days since he'd eaten anything, so he was bringing up mucus and liquor. When he finally finished, he rinsed his mouth out and brushed his teeth. Looking at his reflection in the mirror, he began to cry.

I'm dying, he thought. *I'm dying, and I'm going straight to hell, and I know it*. He began to cry bitterly. Then he remembered that today was Sunday. He checked his watch. It was 8:16 a.m. He could make it to church service. He suddenly wanted to go back to his old church.

As John walked into church, he felt like he wasn't in control of himself. It was like something had taken over and was leading him. He walked past the ushers and took a seat on the back pew. The congregation was reading a scripture:

> I lie in the dust; revive me by your word. I told you my plans, and you answered. Now teach me your decrees. Help me understand the meaning of your commandments, and I will meditate on your wonderful deeds. I weep with sorrow; encourage me by your word. *Keep me from lying to myself; give me the privilege of knowing your instructions.* I have chosen to be faithful; I have determined to live by your regulations. I cling to your laws. *Lord, don't let me be put to shame!* I will pursue your commands for you expand my understanding. (Psalm 119:25-32, italics added)

John bowed his head and repeated, "Keep me from lying to myself, Lord, and please don't let me be put to shame. Amen."

The pastor got up, and John sat up ready to hear him speak. John had always remembered hearing him speak. But the Pastor got up to introduce the speaker for the day.

"Brothers and sisters, we have a treat today. One of our sons has returned! Amen! He was born and raised right here in this church. He sang on the children's choir. The Lord blessed this young man with a tremendous gift for playing basketball. That gift has taken him all over the world: Spain, Greece, Italy, Belgium, and France. He's lived what we call a glamorous life. He's eaten and partied with kings and queens, celebrities and the like; but he found that his soul was not satisfied. Brothers and sister, our son made his way back home. Not back home to us, but back home to God. He recently received his master's of divinity from Jones Theological Seminary and is now an ordained minister. I want you to put your hands together in praise to God as he brings us his word through the lips our or son

Minister Richard Blakely!"

John couldn't believe it. What were the odds that he would come to church today of all days? Rickey? His childhood friend? His first lover? Now a preacher?

Richard stepped up to the pulpit.

"Good afternoon, church. Merry Christmas. Yes, yes. It is Christmas, and we rejoice about the birth of our Lord and Savior Jesus Christ. But we tend to get wrapped up in all the other festivities of the season. You know, this is the time of year we celebrate the birth of Jesus, but his actual birth was during harvesttime, or springtime. So, I'm not going to preach a typical Christmas sermon. I'm going to speak to you today about the Jesus who can turn your life around. Turn with me if you will to the book of Acts: Acts 9:1–7. Let's read together."

> Meanwhile, Saul was still breathing out murderous threats against the Lord's disciples. He went to the high priest and asked him for letters to the synagogues in Damascus, so that if he found any there who belonged to the Way, whether men or women, he might take them as prisoners to Jerusalem. As he neared Damascus on his journey, suddenly a light from heaven flashed around him.
>
> He fell to the ground and heard a voice say to him, "Saul, Saul, why do you persecute me?"
>
> "Who are you, Lord?" Saul asked.
>
> "I am Jesus, whom you are persecuting," he replied. "Now get up and go into the city, and you will be told what you must do."
>
> The men traveling with Saul stood there speechless; they heard the sound but did not see anyone.
>
> Saul got up from the ground, but when he opened his eyes he could see nothing. So they led him by the hand into Damascus.
>
> For three days he was blind, and did not eat or drink

anything.

"Saints, today I want to talk to you about Jesus the Converter. Jesus, the Converter."

John listened as Rich talked about one of his son's favorite childhood movies: *The Transformers*. He talked about how the boy transforms into a machine to help save people.

"Paul was not always a Jesus lover. No, he hated Jesus and those who believed in him. His *job* was to bring the believers to prison. The Bible says that after Steven was stoned, Paul went from house to house, taking men, women, and children to be imprisoned. He hated the believers and made a great deal of money by making sure they were imprisoned. But in the end, God always has his way, doesn't he, saints? Yes. In the end, God's will shall be done. Saul was on his way to Damascus to get some more believers to imprison. He even got a letter from the high priest, granting him permission to take anyone who believed in 'the way' that he might take them to prison. Yes, Paul was on his own mission; he had his own plans. I can see him now, on his way to Damascus with dollar signs flashing in his eyes. He stood to make a lot of money in Damascus, but something happened along the way saints. *God* happened. Paul didn't see it coming either. That's just how God works, isn't it? You never see him coming. But He knows the appointed time in which his chosen will come to him.

"Are you chosen? Has God chosen you today? If you know in your heart that God has chosen you, let him have his way."

The choir stood and began to sing.

"If God is tugging at your heart today—asking, begging, pleading for you to open your heart to him—won't you say yes to him?"

The choir sings:

Open up your heart and tell the Lord Yes
Say yes, yeah yeah

Say I'll obey Jesus, I won't stray Jesus

"My brothers and sisters, Paul never thought he would preach the gospel of Jesus Christ. I never thought I'd be preaching the Word of God! Halleluiah! But *God* had other plans for Paul. And for me. And he has plans for you too. If you just open you heart, surrender your life to him, and let him take control, his plans for you will begin to unfold. It's never too late. There's not a sin that God won't forgive. Come on, brother. Come, my sister. Come, allow the Lord to lead your life."

People began coming out of the pews and walking toward the altar. John wanted to go, but he couldn't stand up.

"Yes, yes! Come, my brothers and sisters. Come all ye who are heavy laden, and God will give you rest. I'm a witness."

There were about ten people lined up at the altar as the choir finished singing.

"Thank you, Lord, for these souls who have come to you today. Saints, the Holy Spirit is telling me that there's at least one more person who wants to come back to the Lord today."

John put his head down. He felt someone touch his back. He turned to see an old, wise face smiling at him.

"Brother, if you want to walk down, I'll walk with you," the gentleman said.

Tears began streaming down Johns cheeks as he nodded. The man grabbed him from under both arms and lifted him up from behind. He took his arm and walked him down the aisle. The congregation clapped and "halleluiahs" rang throughout the church. Richard saw him coming and said, "Yes, brother, yes..." Then he stopped.

"John? john! Halleluiah! Brothers and sisters, this is my child- hood friend from this very church! John Darroff! Yes, brother! Yes! Come! Thank you, Jesus!"

John let the tear roll and began crying uncontrollably as the group accepted Jesus Christ as Lord and Savior and invited him into their hearts. The group was led out of the sanctuary and into a room outside the pastor's office. The church clerk came and gave them forms to complete and asked if they wanted to be baptized. Rickey came in and asked to see John and took him to an empty office across the hall.

"John! How are you? You don't look so good, brother. Tell me what's going on with you."

John told him about Kennedy, and Rickey began to pray immediately for her recovery. Then John told him that he had been diagnosed with AIDS and was afraid of dying.

"Just because you have AIDS doesn't mean you're dying, man. People are living with AIDS all over the world. It's only here in the United States where they give you a death sentence. There are medications available to help you. And you must change your lifestyle. No booze. No drugs. Healthy eating. You went to the wrong doctor. On Monday morning I will personally take you to see a doctor in town whom I know will prescribe the right medication."

"Thanks, man. Listen—" He was interrupted by a knock on the door. A small-framed beautiful, light-skinned woman entered.

"Hey, baby! You were on fire today!" she said before kissing
Richard.

"Thanks, honey. Steph, this is John. John, this is my wife, Stephanie."

Stephanie extended her hand; John shook it. "Nice to meet you,"
he said

"Same here. John? Is this your childhood friend who you used to talk about so often?"

"Yup, that's him! Stephanie and I have been together since I first left Philly. She has been with me through every phase of my life and knows everything there is to know about me. We remained friends throughout her first marriage, and when she got divorced, I asked her to be my wife. By then I had tired of the wild lifestyle I was leading and was in theology school getting my bachelor's. She's been by my side and on my side ever since. She's made a faithful man out of me, John. I barely even look at another woman—or man!" he laughed.

Stephanie laughed too. "That's right! I got him whipped!" Richard laughed. "You sure do, baby. But seriously, that's how the Lord will work on you. When you surrender to his will, he will remove all ungodly desires from your heart. You watch and see, John. God will work things out in ways you cannot even imagine. Now, how about we go to the hospital and see your little girl?"

When they arrived at the hospital, they were informed that Kennedy had been released from ICU, was recovering nicely, and was on another floor. Then they got to her room, Hope and Kamari were there, and they heard laughter. Hope was laugh- ing as Kamari told them a story. Her laughed stopped abruptly when she saw John. John didn't know what to say. Hope looked better than she had ever looked before. He acted as if she wasn't there and went to the other side of Kennedy's bed and kissed her forehead.

"Hi, Daddy. I'm so glad you're here." Hope got up and left the room.

Ain't that a bitch? she thought. *This nigga here is crazy. But I'm gonna be cool. It's all about Kennedy right now.*

"Hey, baby. Hey, Kam. This is my friend Richard. I've known him since we were kids. Went to church today and he was the speaker. I told him about you, Kennedy, and he wanted to come by and have prayer with us."

"Okay, Daddy."

Richard took Kennedy's hand. "Hello, young lady. I'm so glad that you're feeling better. We know God is in control, and every- thing is going to be all right." He looked at John. "Let's all hold hands and bow our heads for a word of prayer."

Hope angrily paced the floor in the waiting area.

"That faggot took me through hell and back, and he has the nerve to act like he has an attitude with me. Like I did something to him. I hate that punk-ass bitch. God, I hate him. Forgive me, but you already know my heart anyway."

She heard the elevator and looked up to see Ed walking toward her. Her heart softened.

"Hey, beautiful!" He grabbed and hugged her tightly. She hugged back just as tightly as tears began to stream down her cheeks. Ed pulled back to kiss her on the forehead and saw the tears.

"Hey! What's wrong, beautiful? Is Kennedy all right?"

"Yes, yes, she's fine. She's in there with her father. When he comes it's like I don't even exist, so I just came out here. It doesn't matter what I do or say. He's always the master of the universe as far as they're concerned."

"Well. Babe, girls feel that way about their fathers. If they were boys, you would be the master of the universe. That's just how kids are. Don't cry. You're too beautiful to be crying."

"But. You don't understand."

She told Ed the whole story about her and John. How he had treated during their marriage and after it ended. When she got to the part about him being gay, she broke down crying again.

"All that time. All that time I thought I was doing something wrong. I thought there was something wrong with me. Then I find out that he just doesn't even like women. Then that made me feel worse. Like there was really something wrong with me. What was it about me that made him hate me—women?"

Ed sat holding her in silence. It was a lot for him to take in. He'd heard of men being on the down low—even in church—but he never actually knew any. He didn't know what to say. It had to be a devastating experience for a woman to go through. He liked Hope a lot. Even though he'd just met her a few short days ago, it seemed like much longer. He realized at that moment that he didn't really know her at all. He wasn't sure if he was ready for all this baggage. But there was something about this woman— something was drawing him to her. Then he remembered the sermon from this morning: "Some things are worth fighting for. Part of being a Christian is being brave enough to address the issues that hurt people, the issues that cause people to not have hope." *Hope*. Then it hit him. This woman—Hope— she's worth fighting for. He pushed back and lifter her head and looked her straight in the eyes.

"Hope. That had to be a pretty rough time for you. It was an awful experience. But look at you! Look at yourself! You are beautiful, vibrant, healthy, and still in your right mind. I know a whole lot of women who would not have been able to endure what you've been through. You are one strong woman. You have to understand now that he is the one with the problem—not you. Obviously he can't even look at you. God only knows what he's had to deal with. Things for him may look all rosy and glamor- ous to you, but you're on the outside looking in. Believe that God is dealing with him. And the girls, don't fault them. They don't

know the truth about their father because you've shielded the truth from them all their lives. And you're still doing it. Now I'm not saying that you should tell them that's he's gay or on the down low or whatever he is, but I'm not saying you shouldn't either. What I am saying is that you have to continue being you. You can't change the past or predict the future. And you can't let him continue to control you."

"He's not controlling me."

"Yes, he is. He's controlling your emotions. Your anger is giv- ing him power. Don't let him steal your joy, babe. You've come too far. And if you allow your anger for him to consume you, you won't be able to let me in. I want you to let me in, Hope. I am *not* John. I need you to let me into your life—into your heart. Can you do that?"

Hope looked him back in his eyes. "Yes. Yes. I can try."

"That's all I ask. Now. Why don't you go to the bathroom and wash your face and get yourself together. You don't want him to see that you're upset."

"Okay." She got up and went to the bathroom.

Ed sat and was getting ready to say a prayer when Kamari came into the waiting room.

"Hey, Mr. Ed! Where's my mom?"

"Hey, Kamari. She just went to the ladies' room." John and
Richard walked in.

"Dad, this is Mr. Ed. Mr. Ed, this is my dad and his pastor friend, Reverend Blakely."

Ed stood up and extended his hand to John, who was taken by surprise, but reached out and shook his hand.

"Nice to meet you."

Then Richard shook Ed's hand. "Nice to meet you, man," Richard said.

"How's Kennedy today?" Ed inquired.

"Oh, she's great! She can move her legs and everything! The doctor said she can come home tomorrow!" Kamari answered.

"Yes, God is good all the time!" Hope heard an unfamiliar voice say as she entered the room.

"Yes, he is!" she agreed as she extended her hand to Richard. "Hello, John."

"Hope."

"So yes, Kennedy is coming home tomorrow. Where are you staying, John?"

"Well, John, you can stay at our house until as long as you need to," Richard chimed in.

"Okay. Thanks. Well, we'd better get going. I'll call you tomor- row, Kam."

"Okay, Dad. Love you." She kissed her dad, and he and Richard left.

They walked to the car in silence, each in their own thoughts. Richard finally broke the silence.

"You look like you need a good meal and a good-night's sleep. Steph is a great cook, and I'm sure she'd love to have you. We have three extra rooms that are unoccupied since the kids are gone. I'll take you to the hotel, you can pack you things, we'll go to my crib, eat, and you can get some rest. Tomorrow I'll take you to my doctor friend and get you the meds you need. God will work it out, brother. You'll see."

"God won't work anything out for me. Not after all the dirt I've done," John whined.

"Brother, my brother. God is merciful and will forgive you, but only if you seek him and ask for his forgiveness in sincerity, repent, and do your best to live according to his will. There is not a sin on earth that he won't forgive. Believe me. I know. I'm a living witness. But you… you gotta make it right with Hope. I don't know all the intricate details, but you do. You need to do whatever is necessary to do right by that woman. Until you do, you will not have peace."

Two Years Later

"Mom, can you get the door? It's probably Daddy and Kennedy. You're not mad that I said I'd ride with them to my graduation, are you?"

"No, Kam. I'm not mad. Ed, baby, can you get the door? I'm still putting on my make-up."

"Sure, babe, but you know you don't need make-up, gorgeous." He opened the door. It was John and Kennedy.

"Hey, man, how you doing? Proud daddy moment today, huh?"

"Yes, yes, it is!" John laughed as he and Kennedy walked in. "Hey, Kennedy! How's your internship going?"

"Great, Uncle Ed! I'm working on a new program for the DOD! I'm learning so much! Thanks again for hooking a sista up!" Kennedy replied as she gave him a big hug and kiss on the cheek.

Hope came down the stairs.

"Hello, John. Kennedy, you look beautiful! I'm glad you liked the dress. It looks really nice on you."

"Yes, it does, doesn't it?" Kennedy said as she did a model turn.

"Thanks, Mommy." She kissed Hope.

"Come on, Kam! We're all waiting for you, daughter!"

Kamari stood at the top of the stairs in her cap and gown. Everyone fell silent, each in their own thoughts.

So much had changed in the past two years. Kennedy was top in her class at Drexel and loved computer technology. Ed sold the jewelry store, and they were about to celebrate their first wedding anniversary next month. He showed her a love that she never knew existed. He taught her the meaning of love and how to love in return. He helped her understand that she needed love in her heart in order to forgive. He also followed his lifelong dream and started his own business as an IT consultant, the same field Kennedy became interested in. Those two computer geeks had become bosom buddies, and Ed even got her an internship at a major IT form in town. Who would have thought that after their rocky start they would turn out to be two peas in a pod?

John told the girls about his lifestyle and shared with them that he had AIDS. He was doing well and looked healthier than he'd ever looked. He sold his half of the Quiznos to his busi- ness partner, Ted, for $350,000 and gave Hope $300,000 in their divorce settlement. He still had money from his severance pay and was working as a project manager for a major construction company in New Jersey. He spent his free time volunteering at a halfway house for men with HIV and was a regional spokesper- son on AIDS. He seemed to have found an inner peace.

It took a lot of prayer and some time, but Hope finally forgave him with her whole heart. He really was a different person, and they learned to at least be cordial to each other. She didn't t know if he still lived a gay or down-low lifestyle, nor did she care. The girls still loved their dad and never talked about his lifestyle or his condition. They were happy to have both parents play an active part in their lives.

Hope paid her brother off his half for the sale of her moth- er's house, and he disappeared. She and Brenda developed a new friendship and talked at least once a week. She was still trying to get her and Ed to come to Dubai. Maybe they would go this year. Patty, Brenda, and Hope formed a coalition and founded a non- profit organization to help women who were victims of domestic abuse and were about to build a new secure facility that would house two hundred women with up to three children.

Life was good. Her journey had been a long one. The road was rough and bumpy, but she had survived. *Only by the grace of God*, she thought to herself. *Only by the grace of God.*

Looking up at her baby who would graduate valedictorian of her class with a full scholarship to Temple to major in criminal justice, she smiled with a mother's pride. She was certainly enjoy- ing this season of her life.